THE BLOOD ON MY SLEEVE

'Matt Kendrick was naïve to the point of folly. The idea was his—a gesture of protest. But it turned sour. Professionals don't go for cultural gestures. He was being *used*. When the police caught him in possession, he became a liability. He was killed because he knew too much.'

Dean Ruskin took the pipe from his mouth and sighed stupefying Albany smoke over me. 'Sordid. I'm truly sorry you found yourself involved in such a sorry affair.' He patted my arm in fatherly fashion. 'Be thankful it's no concern of yours.'

And I believed him . . .

Books you will enjoy
from Keyhole Crime:

THE BLOOD ON MY SLEEVE

Ivon Baker

KEYHOLE CRIME
London · Sydney

First published in Great Britain 1979 by
Robert Hale Limited

Copyright © Ivon Baker 1979

Australian copyright 1981

This edition published 1981 by
Keyhole Crime, 15-16 Brook's Mews,
London W1A 1DR

ISBN 0 263 73556 7

Set in 11 on 12½ pt Times Roman

Photoset by Rowland Phototypesetting Ltd.,
Bury St Edmunds, Suffolk
Made and printed in Great Britain by
Cox & Wyman Ltd., Reading

CHAPTER
ONE

'Trouble?' The bed creaked as Kendrick rolled on one elbow, set his empty glass on a Gideons' Bible by the phone and sank back to stare at the ceiling. 'Nothing I can't handle.'

I glanced round the ten-dollar room with its curtained shower and out at the view—evening sunglow on vast blue-jeaned buttocks in the LEVI'S ad across the street. 'But why *here*? How d'you suppose Myra feels? She wants to help but—'

'Sure, sure.' His feet swung to the floor and he sat with hunched shoulders—defensive . . . foetal—in sweat-clammy shirt and crumpled jeans. 'My charming wife's one idea of help is running back to daddy— back to the great god Foster Norman Durrell.' He lifted his head painfully and peered at me with bloodshot eyes. 'And *boy*!—doesn't daddy just love to be proved right about me? What say, professor—*is* he right?'

'I—'

'No, come on—forget your true-blue British diplomacy for once. Let's have a straight answer. Look at me. What d'you see?'

Behind its heavy defensive moustache his face was still that of the youthful idealist I had tutored seven years before—impulsive . . . emotional . . . vulnerable. I looked in vain—as I had been listening in

vain—for intimations of maturity. He gave me no time
to reply.

'Okay—you don't have to say it. I'm a bum—and of
the worst possible kind. Know what this is? An *intellectual* bum.'

I lifted the whisky bottle from the floor. 'Let's just
say this is making you feel sorry for yourself.'

He snatched it, clumsily tilting the ultimate amber
inch into his glass. 'Spare us the preachment, professor—and don't look so serious. Ten to one—
pounds . . . dollars, you name it—this case never even
gets to a grand jury. The Olivet crowd are realistic.
They've gotten their property back safe, so why make
a martyr out of me? It's like—remember?—that
statue. The one that so mysteriously disappeared from
the Dean's quadrangle. What happened when it came
back? "*Tut! Tut!*" said the Dean. Just that. You won't
find that episode recorded in the annals of British
justice.'

'A student prank, dealt with under college discipline? No comparison. I know precious little about
American law, but I'd guess right now you're facing a
grand larceny charge.'

'Which will never come to court. Put me on the
stand and who knows what I might say?'

Five minutes later I left—gladly. The antique elevator sighed mournfully over my retreat from that ill-starred reunion. Down on street level a merciful
breeze was wafting traffic noises into the shadowed
lobby. At the reception desk a rabelaisian youth regarded me suspiciously from behind a broken-backed
copy of *True Detective*. On impulse I asked to call

Kendrick's room. The gross body sagged forward, one podgy hand sliding a phone in my direction while the other pressed a key on the switchboard.

No reply.

Instead, a woman's scream came cascading down the elevator shaft. High *C* at a guess—and of operatic quality. Galvanised, the clerk tossed aside his book and snatched a snubnose revolver from beneath the desk with fluency of movement suggesting hopeful months' practice for this very crisis. Thus armed, he wobbled across the lobby and made a frontal assault on the stairs, larding the lean earth—Falstaff-wise—as he went along.

By the second flight he was out of the running. I squeezed past his wheezing obesity and headed for the siren shriek on the next floor—where a dough-faced woman in bulging cord pants and pink shirt was pointing dramatically to the open door of 310.

Inside, the room was noisy with splashing water. An abandoned puppet, Matthew Kendrick's naked body lay in the shower, one elbow plugging the drain. The tray ran gin-pink as invigorating spray sluiced blood from his shattered face.

Behind me the clerk's shuddering bulk blocked the doorway while the Rhinemaiden peered over his shoulder.

'Shot', I said, turning off the shower and heading for the door. 'Let's call the police.'

Cue for the most dramatic speech that young man would ever make. His gyrating revolver—ranging in estimated trajectory between my kneecaps and re-productive system—lent weight to his words.

'Mishter'—I swear the classic Bogart lisp was there—'you ain't going *nowhere*!'

A private American dream was dented that evening. Marriage to Anne, with her New England background and Foxdale education, had admitted me to a circle so closely akin to my own that the broad Atlantic seemed shrunk to a river between one English county and the next. Never was I allowed to feel alien—until that hot summer evening in the town of Reverence (*welcomes CAREFUL drivers*).

By a process of deduction beyond my ken but no doubt familiar to readers of *True Detective* young Falstaff held me responsible for Kendrick's untimely death. Hopes that sweet reason might prevail were dashed by the arrival of Officer Muldoon—six feet of dark blue anglophobia garnished with black leather trim and topped by a peaked white dome. His tinted shades flashed hostility in my direction while he listened with maddening patience to a duet of suspicion and accusation from the clerk and the pink-shirted *diva*.

Then he turned to me. 'Okay. Name?'

'Meynell. David Meynell. Listen—'

'Save it. Identification?' He reached out, fingers snapping, chin lifted arrogantly. Only the swastika armband was missing. A quick flash of my official ID wallet might have eased the situation but I had learned caution with the years. My passport was with Anne, fifty miles away. I handed him my British driving licence.

He straightened the plastic folder and glared at the

pale green document. 'Doctor?'

'Philosophy. I'm an archaeologist. Matthew Kendrick was one of my college students back in England, seven-eight years ago.'

He glanced to where water still dripped onto the pathetic body. *'Yeah'*—a slow sigh charged with sinister implications. Compensating for his suspicion, my mind flooded with memories of the Kendrick I had known—all the high promise of those distant student days. He was reading history and my lectures were on the periphery of his studies—almost an optional extra—yet his attendance was regular, questions astute, essays comprehensive if flamboyant in style. Asked for a summary of events leading to the British surrender at Saratoga, he would chronicle General Burgoyne's imagined heart-searchings during his march down the Hudson. My comment, scrawled in red ink on the last page: *C'est magnifique, mais.* . . .

Officer Muldoon was monotoning a high-speed incantation, head tilted slightly like a child reciting a party-piece. I disentangled one phrase: *You have the right to remain silent.* Good idea.

Despite lingering heat, Reverence looked bleak. Viewed from a police black-and-white where I sat handcuffed and seething with silent fury, its deserted, shadowy streets and derelict factories had the pinched look of a Lowry canvas. Only the vast Fairfield Corporation plant evidenced life, with silvered storage tanks sprouting between century-old workshops and a cobweb of gleaming pipes twined about grimy brick walls. In a crowded loading bay men in white swarmed round a fleet of mammoth yellow trucks. As we passed the main gate an ambulance swung onto the road, overtook us and howled urgently into the distance.

Across town at police headquarters I was delivered—a bundle of suspect merchandise—into the hands of a new inquisitor, Brand by name, Lieutenant by rank. Humiliating shackles removed, the contents of my pockets went on public display—spread across the interview room table. Thus did the lieutenant learn whence came my daily bread.

'*Ministry of Defence*? How come you told the officer you're an archaeologist?'

I pointed to my ID wallet. 'Department D19. We deal with all the historic properties used by British armed forces. Castles . . . country houses—even whole villages. That calls for my sort of expertise.'

Not the whole truth—but enough.

'So what are you doing in Reverence?'

'Visiting Matt Kendrick. Hadn't seen him since he graduated. I'm over here for a summer school at Hampton University, lecturing on military archaeology. Check with Dean Ruskin if you want to. Called Kendrick's place this morning just to say Hello. Mrs Kendrick told me he was in trouble and invited me over. I had lunch with her, out on Olivet, then came on down to see Matt. His wife seemed to think it a good idea. I wasn't so sure. I was right.'

'Meaning?'

I shrugged. 'What do you say to an old student who's just stolen art treasures worth half a million—and proud of it? We kept off the subject most of the time. Talked about college, mostly. Depressing. In those days I had high hopes for Kendrick, but. . . .' I left it at that. *De mortuis nil nisi bonum.*

'So—you talked over old times for three hours?' He sounded doubtful.

'He did most of the talking. I'm a good listener, Lieutenant. Just as well. I couldn't offer him sympathy and he didn't want advice. Frankly I was glad to leave. That was just after six-thirty. He was getting ready to lecture at your community college—for the record—when I *did* leave he was alive and well. Not quite sober . . . not quite drunk. Say . . . *belligerent.* But undoubtedly alive.'

He leaned back in his chair and studied a typed report sheet, frowning. When he spoke I caught the first hint of uncertainty. 'I'll level with you, Doctor Meynell. Officer Muldoon walked in on a situation that had maybe, well, gotten out of hand some. The hotel clerk claimed he'd made a citizen's arrest. You have that in England too, I guess. And . . .'—he checked the report—'Miss Wandowska—she found the body—says she saw you coming down in the elevator as she came up the stairs. She'd driven over to take Kendrick to college. Door was open . . . she looked in—you know what she saw.'

'I've explained about that elevator. Couldn't get the thing to work properly. It had me up on the fourth floor, trying just about every button, before it started to go down. That took time. Then I stopped to call Kendrick from the desk. I'd forgotten to give him my address over here. *And* I went back up to his room when Miss Wandowska screamed. That sound like the way a guilty man would behave?'

He placed both hands on the table between us and drummed his fingers briskly. 'Okay—here's what we do: you sit right there while I make a few calls. I'll get some coffee sent in, then we'll hear what you have to tell us. Straighten things out, huh?' At the door of the interview room he paused. 'Dean Ruskin?'

'Or Senator Patterson,' I said blandly. Why not? Patterson owed me a favour.

It was past midnight when I drove up to the saltbox house which was home for us during our brief American visit. Anne met me on the threshold— holding me at arms' length and shaking her head in mock despair. 'Can't I let you out of my sight for *one* afternoon?' The light tone was stretched too taut to cover underlying concern.

I held her close. 'Heartless wench. Is this any way to welcome a man who's endured thumbscrew and rack?'

She lifted her head and gazed steadily into my eyes. 'Wasn't funny, was it?'

'You might say there were overtones of the Keystone Cops . . . but on reflection—*no*, the situation was singularly devoid of humour. Anyone can make a mistake. What got me was the way they did it. Handcuffs . . . frisking . . . "*Turn out your pockets!*". And when they *knew* they'd got the wrong man—Patterson must have given them a rough time—when they *knew* . . . never a word of apology. Just one of those things. Happens every day. Forget it. *Forget it?* No chance.'

She caught my hand and led me into the little parlour—a cosy room still much as her grandparents had known it seventy years before. This was the Dowland family home until Anne's father left to lay the foundations of his flourishing antique business. Here Anne would have lived had she returned from college in England to become Stanley Dowland's partner. But she married me and the house on Brewster Avenue had seen her only twice in the past seven years.

There among sepia photographs, stern portraits and solid antique furniture, events in Reverence slipped into truer perspective.

I squeezed her fingers. 'But what am I moaning about? I'm *alive*. Young Kendrick . . .'

'And Myra—how's she taken it?'

I slapped my forehead. 'Should have called round there after they'd finished at headquarters—but all I wanted was to get straight back here. I'd *had* Reverence. What's she going to think?'

'She'll understand. Anyway, you can explain when you see her.'

'*When* . . .?' It had been a long day and my cerebral cogs were slowing. 'Look my love—deepest sympathy and all that, but you'll not catch me setting foot in Reverence for a very long time.'

She nodded wisely. 'Say three . . . four days? The *funeral*, David. Matt was one of your students. Okay, so maybe that doesn't impose any obligation, but Myra's my friend. I'd have come with you today if it hadn't been for that talk to the Landsbury Ladies. We'll *have* to go.'

Next afternoon I found myself the object of sympathetic interest from those few members of the faculty still in residence at Hampton for the summer school. We met briefly in the senior common room before my lecture on *Archaeological Evidence of the Second World War*.

'Iniquitous!' White-haired Dean Ruskin set a flaring lighter to his bulbous briar and sent tobacco sparks cascading down his jacket. The smell of burnt tweed mingled with acrid anti-social nimbus from smouldering *Albany*—that pungent brand from which the afterhaze lingered long in lecture-hall and corridor as witness to his earlier presence. He drew angrily on the pipe and shook his head, showering more sparks and ash on the carpet. 'Such *insensitivity*! Are we to wonder at the polarization of attitudes in matters concerning law and order? And no apology, you say? Then allow me to proffer one vicariously. Would that I could reassure you as to its being an isolated instance.' Moist hisses sounded from the briar as he puffed pensively. '*Mmm*. And of course it must have been equally distressing for you to discover that one of your former students had set his feet upon the broad way that leads—indeed, that *led*—to destruction. I have experienced similar disappointment all too frequently—never without a sense of personal failure.'

Sally Rackham—Hampton's Professor of European History—was more cheerful. '*Failure* is a relative term, Dean. I guess there's some consolation in the fact that young Kendrick was a most discerning collector. They showed his haul on the midday news. Picasso . . . Monet . . . a Cellini figurine—he knew what to go for. There's a crumb of comfort for you, David.'

Sally had been my contemporary at Oxford in the late fifties. I welcomed her intervention in a conversation which was fast becoming maudlin.

'No cause for pride on my part,' I said. 'If anything, I used to be concerned with curbing his artistic fancy. No need to tell *you* how important imagination is for the study of history—but you've got to start with *facts*. His essays were works of fiction—brilliant in their way but falling apart as soon as you analysed his use of the facts. He was a dreamer . . . unpractical. And that's what worried me.'

'Tread softly,' murmured the dean with a gentle smile. 'This is a house of dreams. It must be—if we're to make sense of reality.'

'I wasn't talking about Kendrick the student. Not that he'd changed much. Claimed he was merely protesting against the obscenity of art investment. Actually planned to exhibit his haul and be damned to the consequences. That I can understand—specially in a town like Reverence. By all accounts the Fairfield Gallery has nothing worth a second glance. But out on Olivet—that's the *right* side of the tracks—the walls drip masterpieces, bought simply with an eye to capital appreciation. No, what bothers me is this unlikely picture of Kendrick the art-thief. Those houses on Olivet aren't easy pickings. Whoever cracked that lot knew all about electronic security systems. Matt Kendrick—he couldn't break into a piggy-bank.'

Sally Rackham peered at me over her goldrims. 'You're saying he had help?'

I nodded. 'The police think so. An out-of-town job. That's one reason I was suspect—a strange face.'

The dean tamped his tobacco with an ash-blackened thumb. 'Professional criminals, eh?' he muttered. 'Your young friend was venturing into deep waters. No place for dreamers.'

'He was naïve to the point of folly. The idea was his—a gesture of protest. But it turned sour. Professionals don't go for cultural gestures. He was being *used*. When the police caught him in possession, he became a liability. He was killed because he knew too much.'

Dean Ruskin took the pipe from his mouth and sighed stupefying Albany smoke over me. 'Sordid. I'm truly sorry you found yourself involved in such a sorry affair.' He patted my arm in fatherly fashion. 'Be thankful it's no concern of yours.'

And I believed him.

CHAPTER
TWO

Funeral?—it was a production number; a scaled-down version of the mortuary pomp beloved of ancient Egypt. Even the gleaming casket with its rich veneer and heavy gilded fittings could have served as a sarcophagus for a pharaoh. The entire performance was staged at a graveside from which all trace of honest earth had been scrupulously removed—hidden beneath a mountain range of potted blooms. Up-centre with a microphone to amplify his eulogy a robed high-priest expounded the virtues of the deceased in tones of cloying professional sincerity. Off-prompt, a choir of earnest women in full academicals hung upon his every word. We lesser mortals—audience rather than congregation—faced star and supporting cast across the apron-stage of Matt Kendrick's lavish coffin. Purple-draped chairs were provided for the principal mourners while the rest stood—like Shakespeare's groundlings, for the most part capable of nothing but inexplicable dumb-shows.

Twin loudspeakers duplicated every syllable of the peroration. *'We-we al-all ha-have goo-good ca-cause to-to re-remember. . . .'* On droned that unctuous voice, quarrying Kendrick's life for rare nuggets of achievement from which to fashion ornaments of oratory.

Unreality engulfed me. Any moment, to rapturous applause, Matt would emerge from behind those massed flowers and smilingly accept his Oscar. A hidden organ throbbed reverent chords and the choir launched into *Rock of Ages*.

His tone still bland and conversational, the Master of Ceremonies brought us to the moment of committal. In his florid vernacular I caught distorted echoes of other remembered funerals—but how bowdlerised the libretto! Gone, Cranmer's majestic prose; banished the King James Version with its rude references to death.

'*A-and so-so we-we lo-lovingly a-and re-reverently la-lay to-to re-rest ou-our de-dear fr-friend. . . .*'

More vibes from the organ and—what's this?—the coffin was sinking from sight! I couldn't believe . . . they had an elevator—an *elevator*!—fitted up beside the grave.

Our borrowed VW was parked a respectful distance from the obsequious black limousines. We walked to it in silence, our footsteps light on the pool-table lawn.

'*Hmm,*' murmured Anne. 'That was . . . *different*?'

'It was awful.'

'It was *terrible*!'

'Not a popcorn seller in sight. What kind of place *is* this?'

She caught my arm. '*Ssh!* They'll hear. But it really plumbed the depths. Poor Myra! And half Reverence is here. I hadn't realised Matt was so popular.'

'He wasn't.' I opened the car door and felt an oven-blast of hot air on my face. 'That's what a bullet does for you. *Nothing in his life became him like the leaving it*. Morbid curiosity. Back there I couldn't help re-membering. . . .'

A tiny knot of mourners round an open grave on a Welsh hillside.

'I know.' She slid into the seat beside me. 'Last time. That was a bullet, too.'

The limousines were moving off. 'You married a bird of ill omen.'

'A solemn owl.'

'I'm serious. I visit a man I haven't seen for seven years and *phht*!—somebody blows him away.' Behind us the engine clattered into life as I turned the key. 'One consolation—you can't blame my job for *this* one.'

We could joke about it now. Back in 1960—fresh from Oxford—I had been recruited into Department DHR2—*Defence—Historical Research (Armed Services)*. An archaeologist's technique differs little whether he is examining an iron-age site or the re-mains of a crashed B17 Flying Fortress. In ten years with the Ministry I saw few iron-age relics but scores of shattered aircraft, tanks, subs—and fully a legion of disinterred warriors.

Solve an archaeological mystery and you may con-found your peers and impress the public—unless you work for DHR2. The fruits of our research passed to the Director, a man never confounded or impressed. That portrait of Wellington surveying the field of Waterloo, twenty years after the battle . . . Know it? It epitomises our work. In the wake of long-disbanded armies we moved across the world's battlefields years after the last shot had been fired. Among grim wreckage of wartime disasters we sought answers to old questions; probed old wounds; uncovered old scores awaiting settlement.

No statute of limitation on treachery. Men, women—grown secure in lives purchased with betrayed blood—found themselves brought to the reckoning.

And sometimes—how shall I put it?—*we settled out of court*. From his desk beneath a Churchill portrait the Director would issue orders; D10 would issue off-the-peg identities; the duty armourer would issue hardware and we would issue forth through the back door, bound for Birmingham, Beirut or Berlin.

Ten years of that, then *out*—my empty desk a monument to government economy. I wandered the wilderness awhile, wangled a Chair of Military History in a northern university—and met Anne. By the time we married I was back at the Ministry and she *persona grata* with the Department. But on our working honeymoon in Istanbul I hindered the passage of a bullet. Result: transfer to D19—*Defence Lands Conservation (Sites and Buildings)*. A sinecure, say you? Not so. The mixture as before—with Anne growing more tense as time passed.

So to that grave on a Welsh hillside. I rebelled. The Director tore up my resignation . . . offered me a cigar and a future free from extraneous duties with time to work at my long-delayed doctoral thesis. I declined only the cigar.

At the house of mourning restrained conviviality prevailed. Refreshments were being served on a formal lawn, secluded between mature box hedges. No place here for the herd—those community college students and Fairfield workers who had snatched a brief hour to attend the burying. This was the elite of Reverence—the Olivet set. Watching Myra Kendrick as she moved among them I felt a chord vibrate in my memory. *Formal attire . . . deferential greetings from the guests*—of course! This was the atmosphere of a Palace garden-party. *O death, where is thy sting?* Not here. These people were making no attempt to disguise grief; they had none to hide. No choked reminiscences of the dear departed. It was as though the grave had engulfed Matt Kendrick's entire existence and all remembrance of it. Beside me Anne was deep in animated description of our Royal Jubilee celebrations for the benefit of a bluerinse *aristo*.

'Doctor Meynell?' A tall man with iron-grey hair and disturbing shrewd pale-blue eyes. Sixty? Maybe more—the upright military figure made age difficult to judge. He leaned forward and spoke confidentially. 'We haven't met but I've heard a great deal about you. I'm Walter Cornhill—Mrs Kendrick's attorney.' We shook hands and he led me a few paces away from the nearest group. 'I'd consider it a favour if you'd spare us a few minutes of your time. Some of my associates are foregathering in the house and we'd value your advice on a rather delicate matter.'

I set my empty glass on an ornate white wrought-iron table. 'Lead on.'

He glanced round the company, smiling . . . nodding at acquaintances while his questing eyes scanned the enclosing hedge. 'Let me urge circumspection,

Doctor. We are, as they say, observed. I'll leave you in a moment. Give me five minutes and then join us in the library.' He stepped back and—for no apparent reason—laughed. 'Indeed yes,' he barked. 'Glad to have made your acquaintance, sir.' Then he was away, mingling with the other guests.

I turned to find Myra watching me—her calm features radiating mature beauty. Widow-black, her simple dress enhanced the burnished copper of her hair. She reached out and clasped my hand with her cool fingers. 'Thank you for coming. I really do appreciate your being here.'

'I owe you an apology. The other evening—'

'No.' She shook her head. '*I* should be the one to apologize—involving you in this wretched business. And . . . the way the police treated you! Don't worry—they haven't heard the last of it. By the time Walter's through with them they'll be grovelling.'

'Please—don't make an issue of it. No need to antagonise them on my account.'

'*Antagonize!*' The word sliced through murmuring conversation. Curious glances turned in our direction. She lowered her voice. 'Walter's asked you?'

'What's the problem?'

Her gaze wandered the garden as Cornhill's had done. 'They'll explain. I'd better circulate. Mustn't focus attention. . . .'

When she had gone I prised Anne discreetly from the bluerinse. 'Suddenly I'm popular. Invited to a furtive assignation—in the library, no less.'

She lifted one eyebrow. '*Myra?*'

'Her attorney.'

'Don't sound so disappointed.'

'You misjudge me. 'Tis not disappointment that clutches at my vocal cords—'tis mere perplexity. He wants my advice. In what capacity?'

She frowned. 'He knows you're with the Ministry?'

'Says he's heard a lot about me.'

'Then watch out. He's probably working for Fair-field.'

'So?'

'Oh come on, David. The word is they make all kinds of unpleasant stuff for the Defence Department over here. Could be they see you as their British Connexion.'

'Ho ho!'

'Just be careful.'

I sauntered towards the house. Beyond the box hedge a familiar figure was self-consciously minding its own business. Lieutenant Brand.

For a man gainfully employed in lecturing at a community college, Matthew Kendrick lived in considerable style. The house—Queen Anne to English eyes—was of warm red brick. Less than fifty years old, its ivy-clad façade gave an illusion of antiquity. Within, the architect's hand had faltered. In the wake of a white-jacketed servant I crossed the chequer-board marble of a baronial hall complete with soaring Tudor staircase, passed through a lofty mirrored Regency salon and came to a low-ceilinged mediaeval library. As we paused at the door—'*English?*' The voice was scornful. 'An *archaeologist*? This is crazy! He won't know—' A warning cough brought instant silence.

We went in. Book-laden shelves projected from the walls to form deep alcoves. In the furthest—by a diamond-paned casement—five men were seated at a refectory table. Walter Cornhill rose to introduce me.

Vincent L Goring, septuagenarian president of Fairfield Corporation—his lined face that of a man who has known hard times. The hand outstretched in greeting bore ancient scars and lacked a forefinger.

Paul Chaimer, Vice-President—forty? . . . deceptively boyish features . . . compulsive grin. His instant use of my Christian name raised the hackles of my Anglo-Saxon propriety.

Grant Aitken—fifties, stout, swarthy—habitually grooming his heavy moustache with nervous nicotined fingers. Bloodshot brown eyes and a head of raven-black hair patently not his own lent him the air of a down-at-heel actor. Born to worry, he was Fairfield's chief financial adviser. As he spoke I recognised the voice I had heard at the door.

I guessed the identity of the last man by his marked facial resemblance to Matt's widow. Foster Durrell, Myra's father—early sixties but radiating the *machismo* of a younger man. Arched eyebrows—matching his daughter's—gave him the appearance of a good-humoured interrogator.

A couple of half-smoked cigars lay crushed in a glass ashtray. If the length of cigar a man discards is the measure of his affluence, I was in the presence of considerable wealth. The room reeked of it. As we settled in high-backed chairs—each fit to serve as a bishop's *cathedra*—eyes turned expectantly towards Vincent Goring, acknowledged senior in years and position. Elbows on the table he tapped stubby finger-tips together as if deliberately emphasising the mutilation of his right hand.

'Doctor Meynell'—the voice was soft and husky—'I guess you have no very high regard for our local Police Department. That gives us something in common. Excess of zeal I'll tolerate only if it produces results. We don't pay our guardians of law and order to hassle an honoured guest.' He inclined his head in my direction.

'As far as I'm concerned the whole episode is best forgotten.'

'Magnanimous of you, Doctor—but don't be in too much of a hurry to forget. It's important that you remember what Matt said to you, that afternoon. No—'—he forestalled my interruption—'—bear with me a moment. We're not prying. Our concern is solely with his latest anti-social exploits. We have our reasons.'

Easy to guess what those were. I recalled Matt's bitter strictures on the Olivet crowd. 'You're the people he robbed?'

Goring nodded slowly. 'A thoroughly distasteful experience, Doctor. We were Matt's neighbours. Business associates too—before he joined the bleeding hearts. Friends?—no, I'll not insult your intelligence by suggesting *that*.' He lifted a slim document case from the floor beside his chair and slowly unzipped it. 'The man was a fraud; a—what's that word, Paul?'

'*Poseur.*' Chaimer spoke as one accustomed to providing *mots justes*.

'Sure—a poser. All that concern for the welfare of Reverence! He'd talk about Fairfield Corporation like it was the Mafia! And just where would this town be if we pulled out? We're the only major plant still operating here. Matt knew the score—but what did he do? He quit! Walked out on Fairfield and made a big number of becoming just a *humble* teacher down at the community college. The champion of the proletariat—but with a house on Olivet. That's what I call co-existence! I guess you've already figured this wasn't his place at all. It's Myra's.' He opened the document case and pulled out a colour photograph. 'Take a look at that.'

I twitched new black-rimmed glasses from my breast pocket and self-consciously slipped them on. Prolonged study of faded mediaeval manuscripts for my thesis had left me unable to distinguish fine detail—but I still resented the need for optical help.

Sally Rackham was right—Matt Kendrick knew what to go for. The picture was a flash shot of his haul. No attempt at artistic effect: a blue-period Picasso woman leaning cosily against an impassive ikon; wary eyes—a Van Gogh peasant—peering from the shadow of a voluptuous blue, white and gold vase; gleaming as on the day it came fresh from Cellini's workshop, a silver figurine of Triton standing in etched relief before a Monet landscape. . . .

Vincent Goring's thumb jabbed the picture. 'Tom Cook, our District Attorney. That smug expression is a fixture.'

'He has good reason to look pleased.'

'The hell he has!' Paul Chaimer took my words as a

challenge. 'We could have gotten our property back without any help from the police department.'

'True,' agreed Walter Cornhill, his tone precise . . . diplomatic. 'And—with hindsight—that's what we should have done. You see, Doctor Meynell, when the thefts were discovered it seemed that Fairfield was the target. Vincent . . . Paul . . . Grant . . . Foster . . . myself—that's too much coincidence. So . . . was the motive political? Some of our more advanced research has become an emotive issue. Vincent called a conference at his place that Monday morning and it was Matt who suggested a political angle. Said he was sure we'd get a call offering a deal—our property in exchange for aborting our chemical defense programme, or something like that.'

'*Matt* was at your conference?'

Cornhill smiled wrily. 'I know just what you're thinking, Doctor—but that's the way it was. I guess he needed to know how we'd react; what we planned to do. So he staged a break-in right here.' He tapped the photograph. 'That ikon was one of the few things he owned in this house. Myra called her father to tell him it had been taken . . . heard about our meeting—and insisted we invite Matt along.'

I looked round the group in amazement. 'You weren't suspicious?'

Chaimer twisted angrily in his chair. 'Of what? Okay, so Matt was a pain—but we never expected he'd pull a caper like that.'

'But . . . a robbery here makes nonsense of his theory about Fairfield being the target.'

Grant Aitken stroked his moustache. 'Because he'd

quit? You'll maybe find this hard to believe, but it gave the whole scenario just that final touch. The ring of truth. Made us feel we were up against real people—smart enough to pull a big operation . . . human enough to make a simple mistake like not knowing Matt had left the corporation. You've got to remember, it's only a matter of weeks since he walked out on us. We figured this heist was set up months ago.' He pulled a cigarette case from his dark grey suit and selected a kingsize with clumsy fingers. 'Anyway, he said to hold off till we knew what the deal was—and we agreed. But Vincent had other plans.'

'A president's prerogative.' Goring slid the glass ashtray towards his financial lieutenant. 'I don't take kindly to sitting on my butt while other people call the shots. Had to do *something* so I called Dan Peters—a private investigator we've hired a few times. He's good. You'll understand *how* good when I tell you he took just three hours to locate our property. It was stashed in a closet at the community college—a closet to which Matt had access and which he was known to have visited that morning. I talked it over with the others but we figured there wasn't much of a choice. If Matt was innocent he deserved to be cleared. If he was guilty. . . . Either way it was a job for the police.' He shook his head gloomily. 'That was our big mistake.'

What—apart from sympathetic noises—were these barons of industry expecting from me? Through open casements drifted snatches of animated conversation and occasional laughter from the merry mourners. Within the library—silence. I folded my glasses noisily and slid them back into my pocket. 'You're obviously

under the impression Matt told me something important that afternoon—but I've learned more about the
robberies in the last ten minutes than in all the time I
spent with him. He was more concerned with justify-
ing his action.'

Foster Durrell snorted angrily. 'That I can believe.
Cultural revolution for Reverence, huh? Did he mention any names?'

'Accomplices?'

Goring fanned a petulant hand as if to clear my
clouded wits. 'If there *were* any, Matt wouldn't tell
you. But he'd get a kick out of running over the list of
the people he'd robbed. Philistines, he called us—
men who only value art in terms of dollars. The boy's
dead but I still find his intellectual snobbery hard to
forgive. But . . . names. Five of us—and one other.
That's the name we want. Until we get it, we're all
under suspicion. That damnfool cop Brand thinks one
of *us* killed Matt.'

His sense of outrage was a shade unreasonable. The
market was wide open and Brand had every right to
shop around. 'I know how it feels. Does he have a
reason?'

'*Reason!*' Goring seemed on the point of exploding.
He snatched the photograph and brandished it in my
face, his hand trembling. '*That's* his reason!'

CHAPTER
THREE

The VW rocked as I slammed its door and sat drumming angry fingers on the wheel. Beside me, Anne leaned forward to ease new black shoes from shapely but suffering feet.

'I'm listening,' she prompted, flexing emancipated toes.

I jerked a thumb at the Kendrick residence, screened by discreet hedges from the garage forecourt where we were parked. 'Know what all that was about? They think I'm some kind of private eye. Fifty dollars a day plus expenses, or whatever the going rate is.'

'You're kidding!'

'My very words—but old man Goring was deadly serious. And where—I hear you ask—did he get such a crazy notion? *Senator Patterson*. You'd think—you really would *think* a man in his position would know the meaning of discretion. He's head-man on a Senate sub-committee which has dealings with Fairfield Corporation. Knows Goring well. Calls him up the other evening. *"What's all this I hear about your cops harrassing my old buddy David Meynell?"* Bends Goring's ear with a highly-coloured version of what happened two years ago and leaves him with the clear impression I do freelance sleuthing on the side—an opinion endorsed by your dear friend Myra. Remember, she was at college when you and I were digging up that Heinkel and getting shot at for our pains. And right now, Goring and his friends need an investigator who knows his way around England. *"Name your price, Doctor."'*

Anne's blue eyes were round with amusement. 'I wish I could have seen your face. Hey—' She gripped my arm. '—you didn't say Yes, did you?'

'For heaven's sake—do I look like a man who's said Yes?'

'*Well* . . . I've seen you this way before when you've been talked into something and then had second thoughts. It's always somebody else's fault.'

'Thank you for that vote of confidence in my powers of resistance. As it happens, I told them you'd kill me if I took the job.'

'You *didn't*!'

'I didn't. I put on my best *hee-haw* Whitehall voice and said the Department doesn't allow extra-mural activities. That satisfy you?'

'Oh sure. The point is—does it satisfy *you*?'

Our tyres crunched across the neat gravel forecourt towards the leaf-shady drive. High hedges allowed no warning of the dark green Cadillac which suddenly zipped across our line of vision from right to left, heading for the elegant wrought-iron gates. Even above the din of our engine I heard the squeal of its tyres as it slewed onto the road and sped away in the direction of town. At our more sedate pace we followed and twenty minutes later were on Highway 89, heading for Concord and the home-stretch beyond.

Behind us the sun sank lower, striking sparks off the windshields and brightwork of cars speeding towards it.

Anne switched on the radio. '—*the one that I want, Ooh!—ooh!—ooh! . . .*'

'Purely as a matter of interest . . .' I kept my tone casual—'ever heard of Oberon Spreight?'

I knew she was watching me. 'Uhuh. Purely as a matter of interest he happens to be one of daddy's biggest customers. Rich . . . a dedicated collector—and a dirty old man. Lives over Brunswick way.'

'Antiques expert?'

'Within limits. French . . . you know—*Louis Quinze . . . Louis Seize.* Furniture . . . paintings . . . porcelain . . .'

'Hmm.' I was remembering that coloured photograph.

'Do I get to know what all this is about?'

I shrugged. 'Your dirty old man has started a witch-hunt in Reverence.'

She switched off the radio. 'Oberon? But he hardly ever leaves home. Hasn't been to a saleroom in years. That's how daddy got to do business with him. Commission-purchasing. He's not the only one, of course. I guess there must be five or six dealers who could put up a *By Appointment To Oberon Spreight* sign.'

'Then if I told you this home-loving old gent flew across to Reverence the other afternoon just to visit police headquarters and run his rheumy eyes over Matt's collection of art goodies . . .?'

'Of course, this wouldn't have anything to do with

the investigation you're not interested in—now would it? Silly question.'

'*Academic* interest—you wouldn't deny me that, surely?'

'*Huh!*'

'Spreight wanted to identify a porcelain vase—one he's been lusting after for years. Caught a brief glimpse of it on the news the other day—enough to get him aloft in a chartered jet and heading west over the White Mountains, cheque-book in hand.'

'That sounds like Oberon. When he's after something, it's all systems go. About as much finesse as a bulldozer. Wouldn't bother him that the vase is evidence in a murder case—somebody's treasured possession. At times he's like a spoilt kid. *Oberon wants!* Yes—and Oberon usually *gets*. That the way it was?'

I shook my head. 'Problems. Oh, he identified it— or claims he did. But when he asked to be pointed in the direction of its owner there were red faces at headquarters. They checked their records and suddenly realised nobody had claimed that particular item. At which point old man Spreight got decidedly tetchy and demanded action—so they called up Vincent Goring and the rest. Blank looks all round. Each assumed it belonged to one of the others. Spreight chuntered about a conspiracy of silence. Brand—you know, the lieutenant—whipped him across to the local DA and that's when the trouble *really* started. Spreight bombarded the DA with details of that vase's *provenance*—all highly technical and, unfortunately, very convincing.'

'Unfortunately?' She seized on the word.

'He sold the DA a new motive for Matt's murder. Up to that moment the police believed Matt was killed by an out-of-town professional to stop him revealing the names of his accomplices. That's still my opinion for what it's worth, but li'l old Oberon says nobody in Reverence can possibly have any title to the ownership of that vase. Stolen, says he, long before Matt got his hands on it. Pinched from one of England's stately homes, would you believe? That suggests somebody wasn't prepared to risk Matt taking the stand in court and betraying guilty secrets. Now since Matt's merry little jest was confined to Olivet—more particularly to people with Fairfield connections—the DA figures *that's* where the killer is. Hence the indiscreet presence of Lieutenant Brand at the funeral.'

Anne was silent for a couple of minutes while the south slopes of Rollins marched past, away to our left. Then she switched on the radio again as if the subject of our conversation no longer held her attention. 'Know what I think?' she murmured. 'Oberon Spreight is up to his tricks again. He just loves fishing in troubled waters. That way he lands his best catches.'

'While a lot of innocent people suffer unwelcome attention from the police. That ain't funny, lady—as I have good reason to know.'

Thursday. Noon. Pattering rain on the lecture-room window prompted a question about English climate. I gathered my notes and slid them into the green folder ON WHICH *MOST SECRET* was only partly obliterated by a reseal label inscribed *HAMPTON LECTURE 5*.

'We don't have *climate*—only weather . . . and that's the same as American.' I paused. 'Only . . . there's more of it.'

They must have heard that one before but it got a laugh. The Summer School was a new experience—anticipated with misgivings. I doubted my ability to hold the attention of students ranging in age from thirty to seventy-five. Past professorial endeavours—not the happiest memories—had left me unprepared for the enthusiasm which greeted my Hampton lectures. These people would soon cross the Atlantic to explore the military antiquities of Britain—hill-forts . . . Roman barracks . . . Norman castles . . . mediaeval battlefields . . . civil war emplacements . . . Napoleonic defences—right down to the relics of World War Two. They were not avid students of matters military but their sense of history demanded satisfaction beyond the well-worn tourist trails to London and Stratford upon Avon. This demand was being met by an enterprising operator working in collaboration with educational bodies in America and England—with David Meynell, sacrificing his annual leave, as part of the package.

An earnest matron was waving. 'Doctor Meynell—should my husband wear long-johns over there?'

Dean Ruskin hammered his pipe against an ashtray as a judge pounds his gavel. A steaming dottle of soggy Albany bounced across the table in front of my reading-desk. Retrieving it swiftly he rammed it back in place with a practised thumb. 'I hesitate to interrupt the flow of these fascinating questions,' he said benignly, 'but the summons to the fleshpots has already gone forth. We'll stand adjourned until this evening.'

A shepherd before his flock he led the way from the room, leaving me to collect scattered photographs and maps used to illustrate my lecture.

'Doctor Meynell?' The man by the door was in his thirties—tall, dressed with casual good taste in a light brown suit. As he came towards me I noticed the slight limp. 'You won't know me, sir. The name's Peters. I'm from Reverence and—'

'*Dan* Peters?'

A warm smile spread across his tanned face. 'That's me. Licensed investigator. They tell me that's something you don't have, over in England.'

'They tell you correctly, Mr Peters.' A mission of gentle persuasion merited no encouragement.

'Spare me a few minutes?'

I glanced at my watch. 'Ten. Punctuality's the politeness of kings but the obligation of guests where college meals are concerned. Sit down, Mr Peters. Tell me what I can do for you.'

He dropped awkwardly into one of the students' chairs, his left leg thrusting stiffly from the hip. 'I'd appreciate your help, Doctor. Coming from me, you'll know it has to be about Matt Kendrick's killing.'

'Mr Peters, I'm leaving for England tomorrow. I already explained to Mr Goring—the nature of my work doesn't allow freelance detection, no matter how generous the incentive. In any case—even if I *could* accept his commission—it would waste my time and his money. Oberon Spreight's a devious character who's stirring up trouble. He wants that vase, so he's dreamed up that tale about it being stolen from an Englishman—a conveniently *anonymous* Englishman —and ending up in Reverence. It's a ruse—aimed at flushing out the legitimate owner so Spreight can make him an offer. Your police in Reverence are adept at jumping to wrong conclusions but they'll soon get back to their original theory. Kendrick was killed by one of his accomplices.'

He was shaking his head slowly, as if pained by the prospect of contradicting me. 'Guess you won't have heard. This wasn't a professional job—not the way you mean. Sure, Matt had help—but if you think he'd gotten involved with a big organization, forget it. One man—that's all—and he wasn't hard to find. The community college—did you get to see it while you were in town? No—I guess you had other things on your mind. Does a swell job but one thing's for sure— it's not Yale. Most of the students are way over the age you'd expect. Service veterans . . . married ladies with time on their hands . . . ex-cons, even. Seemed a good place to start looking. That's where the loot was stashed. So I checked—and there he was . . . little Ollie Piper. Like meeting up with an old friend. I busted him six years ago when I was with the police over in Boston. He's been out and back inside again since then. Lieutenant Brand pulled him in, soon as Matt was arrested, but no dice—the little guy had an alibi and they weren't getting anything out of Matt. So Ollie was sitting pretty. Then—*plup!*—Matt's dead and all of a sudden Ollie's world starts falling apart. Found him in a room over on Selburn. Time I got to him he was already ninety per cent proof and rising. Didn't have to lean on him too hard. Hell, I felt sorry for him.'

'He actually told you he was Kendrick's only accomplice?'

'Sure. And the way he described the m.o.—all the little details—he had to be telling the truth.'

'So where did that vase come from?'

Peters rubbed his stiff leg as if it suddenly troubled him. 'We all make mistakes, Doctor. Just that once I was too eager. He figured I must be after something special—and that meant the chance of a deal. So— promises, promises. First he showed me a picture of the vase from an old newspaper. Found it inside the thing when he took the lid off—so he said. I believed him. That was just typical of Ollie. Gets himself an alibi and then risks blowing everything because of a scrap of paper linking him with the vase.'

'But worth it, if it helps clinch a deal. What did he want—in return for telling you where he stole the vase?'

'Straight insurance. Enough money to get him a long way from Reverence.'

'Reasonable.'

He smiled. 'There are words a man in my position doesn't want to hear—like *assisting a criminal to avoid arrest*. I'll bend the rules . . . look the other way— anything except put my license at risk. So I went back to my office and called Mr Goring at the Kendrick house. This was yesterday afternoon. He was just through talking with you, so I'd picked a bad time— but he ended up seeing things my way. I gave him

Ollie's address and said to call me back if he had any further instructions. Caught me just as I was leaving for home, to say would I get Ollie to call his office number at nine last night.' His fingers drummed a little tattoo on his broad thighs. 'I couldn't do that.'

'Professional ethics?'

His eyes seemed to be searching mine. 'Somebody got to Ollie first. *Plup!* Thirty-eight, by the look of things. Very close range. That sound kind of familiar?'

I nodded. 'You actually discovered the body? I mean, you were the first there?'

'Looked that way—so I had to report what I'd found. But I figured it wouldn't do any harm to take a quick look around.' He slipped a hand inside his jacket and brought out a slim envelope. 'See if that tells you anything.'

I held it for a moment. 'This is evidence. What about all those high-sounding principles . . . the risk of losing your licence?'

'That's *my* problem. Evidence has to be interpreted. That's why I've brought it to you.'

I opened the envelope and slid its contents onto the table. A press cutting and one sheet of blue handmade notepaper covered with the bold scrawl of a confident writer. I reached for my glasses. The blurred press photograph did scant justice to its subject.

RECORD PRICE FOR
POMPADOUR VASE

Recent trends towards lower price-levels in the New York auction market were countered yesterday at the

Knoll-Bertrand Galleries. Georgian furniture maintained the enhanced value it has enjoyed since the war, though many potential buyers were clearly unprepared for the rapid run-up to $9,500 which secured a carved mahogany break-front bookcase with architectural pediment, attributed to Thomas Chippendale III (1779–1820). This piece was purchased by Mr Alistair McCoomb of Dallas, Texas. The price, confidently regarded as a record for this sale, was soon eclipsed by the $11,000 bid for the 'Pompadour' vase (picture above).

There followed a brief description of the vase and a respectful reference to its new owner. Across the cutting someone had penned *N.Y. Times* and a date which showed that thirty-one years had passed since the record-breaking cheque was signed.

By Oberon Spreight!

CHAPTER
FOUR

Rain-wet asphalt paths steamed in the hot afternoon sun as Anne and I strolled towards a chain of ornamental lakes separating academic from athletic on the Hampton campus. Behind us, grey stonework—ahead, deserted tennis courts and sports arena.

I was being called to account.

'David—you *promised*.'

'What was I to do? He'd driven all the way from Reverence. Least I could do was hear what he had to say.'

'This Peters must be some talker. When Vincent Goring asked for help, you turned him down.'

We paused on a narrow bridge, leaning over the stone balustrade to gaze at our reflection in the still water.

'That was different. When Goring talked to me—what was the situation? Oberon Spreight was claiming the Pompadour Vase had been stolen in England. Peters has a contact in the DA's office and according to that source, Spreight wouldn't be more specific. Just . . . *England*. Looks small on the map, but it's a hell of a lot of ground to cover. Goring expected me to find out where, when, how—the lot. Ridiculous. Today it's different. We have a lead. And Peters said *'Please'*—something Goring omitted to do. So I agreed. I wish you'd met Peters. He improves on acquaintance. Modest enough to admit he'd be out of his element in England.'

She gave a sigh of exasperation. 'You're hopeless! Sure he was modest. That way he's got you doing his work while he pockets Goring's fee. And what's this lead? So far you've only told me Oberon Spreight bought the Pompadour Vase, back in nineteen forty-seven.'

For answer I showed her a photocopy of the letter Peters had found.

DANTON COURT
Imberbridge
via Rugby
Warwickshire

Thursday

My dear Effendi

Feeble 'Hoorays' from my sickbed! (A summer chill, no more—but troublesome when you're well past the threescore years and ten.) So the Axis begins to crumble, with Marshal Baggy-dolio leading the way. Had we but known, I'd have plundered the cellar for festive tipple. At least—unwittingly—we honoured the occasion with a full-dress turnout. You looked splendid in the old British scarlet (no—not 'redcoat', dear boy!) and I must say it fitted you better than me after all these years.

A request—possibly superfluous. I'd be grateful if you wouldn't mention 'Pompadour' (verb.sap.) to anyone. It's one of the few things left from the old days and the less people know about it, the better.

When you're this way again, drop in.

Sincerely *H.A.*

Anne's fair eyebrows drew together in a puzzled frown. 'It's like listening to half a conversation on a bad line. Somebody—initials *H.A.*—is anxious about something called the Pompadour, which I guess *has* to be the vase.'

I turned and leaned back against the balustrade, feeling the sun hot on my shoulders. '*H.A.*—tell me about him.'

She spread the photocopy on the stonework and bent to study it. '*I see a dark stranger!* English. Wealthy—no, he's *been* wealthy but maybe now he's just keeping up appearances. Old. In the army as a young man. He's big . . . and jolly, like. . . .' She snapped her fingers. 'You know—the actor. *Morley*. Robert Morley. That's how I see him. How'm I doing?'

'Holmes, you amaze me!'

'I'm not through yet. *Effendi*—the word's Turkish, sure, but it's obviously a nickname. He's American. That crack about redcoats—it's the sort of thing you used to say to me.'

I smiled at the memory. 'In your wild colonial days. Care to hazard a guess at the date this was written?'

'World War Two for sure. *The Axis begins to crumble*—that would be when? D-Day. Forty-four?'

'Marshal Badoglio took over in Italy when they booted Mussolini out and surrendered. That was a year before D-Day. So *H.A.* owned the Pompadour Vase in forty-three. Four years later Oberon Spreight bought it at the Knoll-Bertrand Galleries. Now—for reasons best known to himself—he says it was stolen in England. Could he be telling the truth? Did he sell it again?'

She shook her head slowly. 'Unlikely. Like I said—Oberon *wants* . . . Oberon *gets*—and Oberon *keeps*. But you'd better not take my word on that. I'm out of touch with the trade. Daddy could check it out if you think it's important. Hey—but you said Oberon went to Reverence because he wants to *buy* the thing. I can't see him doing that twice over—not without a very good reason. Anyway, just what exactly have you agreed to do for Mr Private Eye Peters?'

'Very little. Find out who *H.A.* is—or *was*—and what happened to the Pompadour Vase. Shouldn't take long.'

She gave me a pitying look. 'David Meynell, you're hopeless. If you didn't have me to look after you, you'd be scampering around England wasting your time on a job I can do in fifteen minutes flat, right here and now. I'll call Knoll-Bertrand and ask them to check their records. They'll have the full *provenance* of the Pompadour Vase. When was that sale?'

'The press report was dated October the first, nineteen forty-seven, and the sale was the previous day. *Thirty days hath September*. . . .'

'Right—let's get to a phone.'

It took her a lot longer than fifteen minutes and when she found me in the SCR, checking notes for my evening lecture, I knew by her sidelong glance that in some way soon to be revealed I was at fault.

'*October one*,' she said silkily. 'That *is* what you said?'

'Problems?'

'Oh *no*!' A deep breath. 'No problems—except that I've been making a complete fool of myself and wasting Knoll-Bertrand's valuable time by insisting—in spite of their politely-expressed doubts—that the Pompadour Vase was sold on September thirty. Where's that cutting from the New York Times?'

I handed her the photocopy Peters had left. She took one look and slapped it on the table in front of me. 'As I thought. Look!'

I looked. *N.Y. Times. 1–10–47.* To err is human. I smote my breast in penitence. '*Mea culpa!* I know, I know—I should have learned by now. If I'd seen that date on a letter I'd have turned it round and translated it into English. But seeing it like *this*—in isolation—I just read it with my poor old insular eyes and it came out October the first.'

'Whereas a *child* can see it says January ten. I mean—*really*! That's what it *says*. So the sale was on the ninth—which is where they eventually located it. Anyway—here's what you want to know.' She consulted a scrap of paper. 'The vase was originally a royal gift to Madame de Pompadour, fashioned by Tournier—'

'Skip the technical details—just tell me who *H.A.* is and when he sold it.'

'No can do. It belonged to an English family for over a hundred years, but their name was Cobley. They got it from a woman called Coote whose husband stole it.'

'*Stole?*'

'All right—*found* it. He was an English cavalry

captain during the Peninsular war. Wandering round a battlefield in Spain he comes across an abandoned carriage. Inside—the vase. That's *his* story. Unfortunately his lucky discovery doesn't do him much good. Killed, the very next day. Vase shipped back to England where sorrowing widow promptly sells it. Purchaser, Jonas Cobley, gentleman. Price—ten pounds. A latter-day Cobley sold it for *one thousand* pounds in nineteen thirty eight. That's when it came to America. New owner—Theodore Shelling of Boston. Nine years later—January forty-seven—Oberon Spreight gets his clammy hands on it. So you see—no *H.A.*'

Dinner that night was to be a mildly formal occasion marking the end of the Summer School. We were preparing our palates with excellent sherry in the Commonwealth Room—as Hampton calls its JCR—when I was called to the phone. Dean Ruskin's secretary from the college office. 'A Mrs Kendrick on the line, Doctor. Shall I put her through?'

'Go ahead . . . Myra?'

'David.' Her soft voice was scarcely audible above the general conversation. 'I was afraid you might have left for home.'

'Tomorrow. Anything wrong?' Fine question for the widow of a murdered man. 'I mean—'

A gentle laugh. 'Sure, I know what you mean. No—I just wanted to apologize. From what I hear, Vincent was less than tactful yesterday. Sorry I didn't see you before you left but to be honest I'd had enough. I knew he'd planned to ask for your help but it never occurred to me he'd think you could be hired like someone from an agency. I don't blame you for refusing. I just want you to know I'm sorry it happened that way. Now you have a good trip and try not to think too badly of us out here in Reverence.'

'That's very kind of you, Myra—and you can tell Mr Goring I've had a change of heart. Peters was very persuasive this morning. Now we have something definite to work on, I'll do what I can. But don't expect miracles. Danton Court could be a blind alley.' A long silence. 'Myra? You still there?'

'I . . . I didn't get that, David. Peters? What's Peters been doing?'

'He was here this morning—with the stuff he found on Ollie Piper. Or didn't you know about that?'

'Ollie *who*? David, what is this?'

'Piper. The man who was shot yesterday. He helped Matt with his . . . with his *escapade*.' What else could I call it?

'I've heard nothing of this. Anyway, Peters is off the case—as of last night.'

'You mean Vincent Goring didn't send him over here?'

'I'm sure he didn't. They had—well, an *argument* is putting it mildly. Don't ask me what it was about—Vincent wouldn't say. But it ended with Peters being fired.'

'Then what's he playing at?'

'I don't know. Look David, I'll check with Vincent. He'll call you.'

But Vincent L Goring apparently thought otherwise. We left for England without hearing from him.

* * *

Summer had overspent its strength in May. When we reached London that Friday evening in mid-July the sky was overcast and a northeast wind was blowing. Our Kensington apartment offered chill welcome and looked as if it had lately witnessed an orgy. Departure, three weeks earlier, had been hurried and the place bore ample evidence of our sins of omission—clothes scattered in the bedroom, unwashed breakfast things stacked in the kitchen sink, a bottle of rancid milk rebuking us pungently from the table.

We turned on the heating, tidied the place, microwaved a frozen meal, shared a very hot bath, went to bed—and took extreme delight in each other's company for the next hour.

Then Anne said, '*Wow!*'. . . relaxed heavily on top of me—and suddenly it seemed we had never been away.

I glanced at the digital clock radio by the bed. 'D'you realise it's only just after ten? This must be an all-time record for us.'

'In more ways than one.' She kissed me very gently. '*Mmm* but I was ready for that. I don't know about you, but I found the Dowland ancestral bed decidedly inhibiting.'

'And lumpy. I began to suspect one of your forebears was still under the mattress.'

Her warm chuckle vibrated against my chest. 'Those pictures, too. Dear great-grandmama. I'm sure she didn't approve—especially in the afternoons.' She lifted her head and looked into my eyes. 'You all right now?'

'Never better.'

'You know what I mean. You were mad—I could tell. Ever since Myra called.'

'Oh *that*. I just resent being treated like a spare part. Peters . . . Goring—I don't know what game they're playing, but they can get on without me. A plague on both their houses! I've better things to do with my time. You've convinced me that Danton Court, *H.A.* and all the rest have no connection with what happened in Reverence last week.'

'*Ah!*' She raised herself on her hands and gazed down at me. 'Yes . . . well. . . .'

'Oh *no*. Don't tell me. You've changed your mind!'

She tried to look penitent and failed. 'There could be a connexion—but if you're not interested. . . .'

I hesitated. Up to that moment I had been able to feel only annoyance that Matt's killer had involved me in the aftermath of his crime. Now—perhaps because I was back home and could remember more clearly the younger Kendrick I had known here in England; perhaps because the last hour had purged my mind—I felt mounting hatred for the faceless shadow which had crept into that hotel room and wantonly spilled all Matt's promised future into an overflowing shower tray.

'I'll buy it,' I said.

CHAPTER
FIVE

As we drove north through steady drizzle I pondered the wisdom of our enterprise. What had seemed reasonable 'twixt matrimonial sheets the night before, appeared now as waste of time. Paradoxically, shortage of time was the only factor supporting our actions. I had to be back in the Whitehall warren on Monday morning. Just two clear days to put Anne's theory to the test.

Her idea was simple. *Two* vases. If Oberon Spreight paid a record price for a singleton, only to discover it was one of a pair, what more natural than for him to compass heaven and earth to gain its partner. Mere supposition—but coming from someone with Anne's knowledge of antiques and collectors, to be taken very seriously. And with free time at a premium our best bet was to visit Danton Court—last known resting place of the piece of porcelain.

Just north of Blue Boar Services we left the M1 for the M45 in company with a stream of holiday traffic heading for Coventry, Birmingham and the Welsh border beyond. Ten miles further and we were off that pulsing artery, driving along quiet lanes into the heart of England. The clouds marched away to the west and within minutes the sun was shining from a blue sky. At every junction the signs for Imberbridge pointed left and after ten minutes we found ourselves back in the shadow of the motorway. Its high embankment, dominating a shallow valley, was pierced by two arches. One spanned a sluggish stream, the other a narrow road. Northwards the countryside lay hidden beyond that man-made skyline along which sped summer-swollen volumes of traffic. Such was now the fate of once-peaceful Imberbridge.

Nor had the village escaped the hand of the developer who promises rural seclusion but can only supply an extension of suburbia. Clustered around a grey-towered Norman church the ancient heart of Imberbridge retained its dignity, but to the west—in what must once have been good arable land—the fell sower had sprinkled his dragon's teeth and twenty identical brick boxes had erupted from the soil.

Anne pointed to a nameboard. '*Danton Avenue*. Getting warm.'

We stopped by the first house where a young man was strapping luggage on the roof-rack of his car. I wound down the window and leaned out. My question brought a puzzled frown to his face. 'Danton *Court*? No—you've got me there. Sure you don't mean Danton *Close*? That's up at the end.'

'It's the name of a house.'

He shook his head. 'We're all numbers round here. You could try across in the village.' He spoke of it as of a different world.

Turning, we drove a hundred yards, forked right to cross a narrow packhorse bridge and found ourselves among mellow brick and half-timbered houses. It *was* a different world—in which P Hamden was proud to proclaim himself *BLACKSMITH*, adding *Agricultural Engineer* as an afterthought. That he also sold petrol was a secret to be guessed from two museum-piece pumps glimpsed behind his forge. Here too N Bovingdon and Son announced to a deserted High Street that they were *Purveyors of High Class Meat*. Neat white lettering on their window provided further ambiguous information: *FAMILIES SUPPLIED*.

A jangling bell heralded our entrance to the dim interior of Imberbridge's Post Office and General Store. Even before our eyes adjusted to the gloom, a heady mix of smells advertised the more pungent merchandise, tugging my memory back to a childhood before supermarkets and the mania for pre-packaging.

The elderly postmistress smiled at us through a wire grille. 'Danton Court? Haven't heard that name in years.'

'We asked in Danton Avenue,' I told her. 'They couldn't help us.'

'Them 'cross Imber?' She glanced up at the low ceiling and shrugged—a swift eloquent gesture of good-humoured resignation. '*They* wouldn't be knowing. Not been here above a twelvemonth, most of 'em. But you'll not find stick nor stone of Danton Court now. Pulled it down when they were making the new road.' She shook her head and I caught the whisper of a sigh. 'Lovely old place. Just let go to wrack and ruin. Years it stood empty—the drive so overgrown you couldn't get past the gate. Then all of a sudden it's sold. Smart-alec from Birmingham way, so they reckon—gets it dirt cheap, collects compensation when the new road comes through—and then goes and puts up all those nasty little houses, 'cross Imber—right where the kitchen gardens used to be.'

'Brought a bit of trade, though,' I said, encouragingly.

'Huh!' Something approaching a scowl darkened the gentle face. 'Sooner get in their cars and drive to Coventry they would, than walk across here. That—and Co-op vans. Old Mister Annandale would turn in his grave if he could see Danton now.'

Anne said, 'Which Mister Annandale would that be?'

'Why—Mister Hugh, love. There weren't any others. Last of the line he was—with young Master Francis being killed in the war. If it's Annandales you're looking for, I'm afraid the only place you'll find *them* is the churchyard.'

'Exactly when did he die?' I asked, to keep the conversation alive.

'Mister Hugh? Oh—years back.' The old woman rubbed her forehead thoughtfully. 'I lose track of time. It was after the war—that I *do* know. Sad business too, poor old man. He was killed, you know. Murdered. They never did find who did it. Wicked. Talk at the time about one of the Air Force boys being suspected but we reckoned 'twas gypsies. They were for ever poaching on his land when they were this ways about. Mister Hugh he never minded the local lads putting down a few snares, but gypsies he couldn't abide. Course, they all swore black's white none of 'em was near the place that night. But they never came back this way again—not in all the years since. Make of that what you will. Us here in Imberbridge never had any doubts.'

The doorbell clanged as a customer entered. I ventured one more question. 'We're in antiques—trying to trace an item from Danton Court. Was there a sale of furniture and effects?'

The postmistress pursed her lips. 'I can't exactly call to mind—' She appealed to the newcomer—a thickset horsey woman in tweeds. 'There was a sale wasn't there, Mrs Morden? Up at the Court—after Mister Hugh . . . you know. Folk here trying to trace some antiques.'

The woman stared at us with amused interest. 'Ha!' she boomed. 'Going back a bit, aren't you? Must be all of thirty years ago. Yes—there was a sale but . . . *antiques*? Not on your life. Poor old Annandale had sold all his decent stuff. The war hit him hard. Most of the rooms were shut up. Living in the kitchen at the finish. Least—so I heard. Couldn't afford to heat the place—and that winter was shocking. Snow on the ground till past Easter. When was that now? *Forty-seven*. And then we had that marvellous summer. The gardens at Danton should have looked a treat but of course everything just ran to seed. Rotten business altogether. You'll have heard. Gyppos. You'll never have me believing different. Riff-raff. But—where was I? Oh yes, *antiques*. Not a hope. Trying to trace something, eh?' Her eyes narrowed. '*What* exactly?'

Anne and I spoke together. 'A picture.' 'A clock.'

I coughed. 'A picture *and* a clock.'

Anne nodded. 'Picasso—blue period. Seated woman. And the clock's French. Gilt. Very ornate—

with a statuette of a *chasseur*. About *so* big.' I recognised two items from her father's latest catalogue.

'*Picasso?*' The woman threw back her head and whinnied. 'At Danton? Not on your life. Old Annandale had no time for modern nonsense. *The Huntsman's Wedding* was more his mark—and I bought that. But the clock . . . *yes*—that does sound like him. Not that there was anything of that kind in the sale. If it came from Danton he must have sold it years before. American, aren't you?' Anne nodded. 'Well, if that clock's in America, I'm not surprised. Know for a fact he sold quite a few bits and pieces during the war—to Americans. Well, why not? They had the money.' She flashed a quick, false smile. 'Look—if you're interested in Danton Court you can't do better than pay a visit to old Mrs Drumsell over at Croxford. She was Annandale's housekeeper for centuries. You'll find her in the almshouses. Ninety if she's a day—but sharp as a needle. Get her talking about Danton and you won't be able to stop her.'

'*If* it's one of her good days,' cautioned the postmistress. '*And* if she takes to you.'

'Glory, yes!' The horsey woman wagged a warning finger. 'Don't get the wrong side of her. If she thinks you're just nosey-parkering she'll turn cantankerous. Mind you—that's an experience in itself. I've seen her stand up to a great pig-ignorant gyppo horse-dealer *and* send him off with a flea in his ear. She was a real treasure. Loyal as they come. Don't think old Annandale realised how lucky he was.'

'These almshouses . . .?' I prompted.

'Can't miss 'em. Take the road back across Imber

then turn left as if you're going to Warwick. Croxford's about five miles. You'll see the almshouses on the right as you go into the village. What's the time?'

I checked my watch. 'Quarter to twelve.'

'Well, don't arrive before three. They won't thank you if you get there at lunchtime and after that the dear old biddies take their teeth out and have a nap.'

'Where does one eat around here?'

'Depends what you want. Ploughman's lunch at the *Dun Cow* along by the church. You could travel further and fare worse. Otherwise it's Rugby.'

'There's the *Tudor* at Bredbury,' suggested the postmistress helpfully.

The horsey woman snorted. '*That* place! All foreign cooking and waiters who don't understand a word of English. Hasn't been the same since the Todds left.'

I glanced at Anne. 'A look round the village, then the *Dun Cow*?'

As we were leaving, the equine Mrs Morden called us back. 'Just remembered. You *could* see if Tim Brice has anything on Danton. Lives in an old hut just through the arch beyond where the house used to stand. Might cheer him up if you call. He thinks the whole world's against him. He *writes*, y'know.' She made it sound a perversion.

The name Annandale had been honoured in Imberbridge for centuries, as a score of monuments in the church bore witness. Those who survived the tragic infant mortality of bygone ages ranged the world in the service of their country. Long-vanished battlefields still harbour their remains—a leg here, an arm there, elsewhere their bodies entire. They fought with German mercenaries against the French in Canada; with French against Germans at Mons. Under General Sir John Moore they advanced, retreated and advanced again across Portugal and Spain. They brandished sabres at Waterloo and Inkerman; mounted punitive expeditions against Indian mutineers; commanded ranks of volleying rifles in the Sudan. Their womenfolk died in childbed or wore themselves out raising vast families from which came successive generations of officers for the Royal West Warwickshire Regiment. Their marble faces stared down at us as we sat in the cool church discussing our quest. Up in the dim chancel a group of women quietly dusted choirstalls and arranged flowers on the altar.

'Facts,' I said. '*H.A.* was Hugh Annandale. Clobbered in forty-seven. Pompadour Vase not among his effects.'

Anne was idly leafing through a shabby prayer-book. 'Sold earlier—to an American? *They had the money*, remember.'

'Don't take it personally. Anyway, that's conjecture.'

'Mmm. Oberon Spreight paid eleven thousand dollars for his vase. That's *money*. Can you see a man on active service parting with even half that amount in a private deal? Anyway, according to his letter, Hugh Annandale wanted to keep the vase. Said it was one of the few things left from the old days. Didn't want people to know about it.'

By my feet a lean and hungry spider was prowling the Lost World plateau of a red knee-dinted hassock.

Something about it reminded me of Annandale as Mrs Morden had described him—isolated . . . shrunken. 'He *said* he didn't want people to know. But could that have been to get Effendi interested in buying? Make him think he was onto a bargain nobody else knew about?'

Anne shook her head emphatically. 'You want to sell, the trick is to suggest right off that somebody else is interested.'

I kicked the hassock and watched the spider scuttle for safety as a mushroom cloud of dust erupted. 'Could be we're wrong and there's only one vase after all.'

She stared. 'But . . . we agreed—two vases is the only way to make sense of what we know.'

'Unless Knoll-Bertrand got it wrong. All that stuff about the vase being found in an abandoned carriage and sold for ten pounds—how would they know?'

'They'd go by what the seller told them. Theodore Shelling of Boston. But not *just* that. They'd want bills of sale . . . a certificate of authenticity from the maker or an acknowledged expert. Oberon Spreight wouldn't part with eleven thousand dollars without making sure he got the genuine article.'

We were getting inquisitive glances from the direction of the chancel. At the door my contribution to the box marked *CHURCH FABRIC* clattered noisily but earned us nods and smiles. Yea verily, they who practise their piety before men have their reward. Beyond the porch dazzling sunlight welcomed us warmly to the land of the living. Last traces of the morning's rain steamed upwards from the churchyard path. I opened the lychgate and paused with my hand on its weathered oak. 'I'm not questioning authenticity—only how that vase got to the Knoll-Bertrand sale. Theodore Shelling claims he bought it for a thousand pounds in nineteen thirty-eight. Suppose he didn't. Suppose he was over here during the war . . . got to know about Annandale's Pompadour Vase—and bought it. The thing had sentimental value for Annandale but he might not realise its true worth. Shelling was a collector—*he'd* know. Maybe he conned Annandale into parting with it for a ridiculously low figure—then had a twinge of conscience. So when he came to sell, he concocted a tale about buying the vase for a thousand—big money before the war.'

Anne smiled indulgently. 'David there are times when you make me feel positively *old*. You have such childlike innocence of the ways of commerce. *A twinge of conscience?* That'll be the day! If a collector gets something dirt cheap he feels *marvellous*—goes around telling everyone what a smart guy he is. Believe me, the ethics of the antiques business weren't handed down on tablets of stone.'

Humbled, I led the way to the *Dun Cow* and a ploughman's lunch surpassing excellence. An hour later, replete and mellowed, we strolled across the river for a closer look at Danton.

Sole identifiable relic of vanished glory was a stretch of redbrick wall. Fifteen feet high it ran beside the road for fifty yards, ending at a tall pillar crowned with a grey stone ball. Two iron pintles in the brickwork showed where a large gate once hung. Only imagination could bring back the other pillar which must have flanked this entrance to a long-vanished drive—but imagination was distracted by modern houses cluttering the landscape. At its far end the wall tumbled to ruin by the motorway embankment. Through that towering bank burrowed the road thrusting northwards to open country beyond. As though summoned by Hamelin's pied piper we passed that gloomy echoing portal and stood glorying in a view which had changed little in centuries—gently undulating fields ripening to harvest and mature woodland; a chequerboard of varigated greens and browns.

From behind a hedge on our right came sounds of hammering. A few more steps and we were looking over a five-barred gate to where an elderly bald man in check shirt and faded jeans was offering violence to the roof of a wooden hut in the middle of a small triangular field. He appeared to be fixing a strip of black plastic material on the weathered grey slope where he perched precariously. New patch . . . old garment. As we watched, he dropped the hammer and rocked backwards and forwards, clutching his thumb. Unheeded, the hammer slithered down the roof and dropped to the ground.

He caught sight of us as we opened the gate. 'My God!' His stentorian voice battered our ears even at fifty paces. 'Don't you people ever give up?'

CHAPTER
SIX

I retrieved the hammer and held it aloft. 'Mr Brice?'

He glared down. 'You can just take your eviction order, or whatever it is *this* time and—'

I raised both hands in a pacifying gesture. 'We've been told you can give us information about Danton Court.'

'You're not from the Council?' He looked embarrassed. 'No—course you aren't. Not a briefcase between the pair of you. Dear God—*real* people! Don't go away.'

As he edged awkwardly towards a ladder propped against the hut I glanced round his domain—neat rows of vegetables . . . hens pecking and scratching contentedly . . . a couple of tethered goats cropping the grass.

The hut itself was larger than appeared from the road—some fifty feet by twenty, the type of temporary structure thrown up to meet transient military demands. After World War Two hundreds had been dismantled and sold for re-erection as site offices, garden sheds, holiday chalets. Its planked walls were bleached and splitting. One corner bulged outwards and the long roof undulated, its fabric stretched across timber frames like emaciated flesh on the ribs of a starving man.

Brice descended the ladder slowly, blood dripping

from his injured hand. 'Bureaucrats!' he grunted.
'They want to condemn this place. Unfit for habita-
tion.' He slapped his undamaged hand against the hut
wall as a horseman pats the flank of a favourite mare.
A decayed plank promptly slipped six inches to reveal
flimsy internal panelling. Undismayed, he thrust it
back in place. 'Basically sound,' he muttered, hastily
wedging it with a wad of roof felt.

Anne indicated his vegetables and livestock. 'Self-
sufficiency!'

'*Survival*!' He spoke gloomily. 'Came here to
write—ended up a peasant. That's the story of my life.
What's yours?'

She smiled. 'I'm Anne Meynell. My husband
David. He's archaeology, I'm antiques.'

Brice nodded acknowledgment. 'Which of you is
interested in Danton? I mean d'you want its history
or an architectural description of the Palladian gem
they bulldozed five years ago? I can supply both.
Nine months I wasted, researching that place.' He
took the hammer from my hand and led us into the
hut.

A short passage past closed doors opened into a
large room smelling of damp and dogs. One wall—the
end of the building—was lined with books. Dust . . .
cobwebs—no volume had been moved in years. He
brushed the sleeve of his shirt across a couple of
Windsor chairs and motioned us to sit. The only other
furniture was a card table and a canvas deckchair in
which he settled cautiously.

'I apologise for entertaining you in a museum,' he
muttered. 'My *sanctum sanctorum* is along the way—

squalid beyond belief. Once—seems like a former existence now—I used to work in here. Now I've joined the ranks of kitchen-table authors. Ah—I observe the furrowed brows . . . the polite attempts to recall seeing my name on a cover. Thank you, thank you—but relax. You won't have read any of my stuff—unless you're into kids' comics and annuals. All mercifully anonymous.'

'But it used to be different,' said Anne gently.

'Are you *asking* or *telling*?' He glanced up from wrapping a handkerchief round his injured thumb.

'Telling.'

He leaned back and stretched his long legs. 'Ages ago—when you were but a gleam in your father's eye, my girl—I wrote plays. You know—*plays* . . . quaint forms of artistry once presented in mysterious and wonderful places called theatres. *Real* theatres where you sat and waited for the curtain to go up; where actors were clothed and in their right mind—and spoke the speech as the author pronounced it unto them. And because in those far-off days I could move with the times, I wrote for radio. There was a fruitful field for drama known as *Children's Hour*. You won't remember it.'

But *I* did—and suddenly I remembered him. '*Timothy Brice!*' I exclaimed. '*The Grey Walls of England*. I used to listen to those when I was a kid. They were great.'

A smile twitched his lined cheek, faltered—and died. 'You heard them with the uncritical ear of a child.'

'They were written for children.'

'So they were. So they were.' He seemed to be making a great effort. 'Look—you must excuse me. Cynicism has become the anodyne of my declining years. Enough! Let's talk about Danton Court. One moment while I get the bumf.'

He rose carefully from the frail deckchair and shuffled out of the room.

'One of your boyhood heroes?' asked Anne quietly.

'*The Grey Walls of England* made a tremendous impression on me. There were plays about castles . . . cathedrals . . . monasteries. Made history come alive. Okay, so they were romantic, but he'd done his homework.' I looked round the neglected room. 'And now—*this*. What went wrong?'

From a distant part of the hut came sounds of metal and china objects tumbling to the floor—then the shuffling footsteps returned.

'Here we are.' Brice blew dust from a thick sheaf of typescript. 'A labour of love—in every sense of the term. Got damn-all for doing it. Nine months in the making but never brought to birth. Look at it! Know what it is? No—course you don't. This was to have been a new roof for the parish church.'

It was a *Son et Lumiere* script—the history of Danton Court, to be broadcast through stereophonic speakers while special lighting effects played on the building itself. A former rector of Imberbridge had conceived the idea after watching a similar production at a French chateau. In those days Timothy Brice was still remembered as a radio dramatist and it was in the book-lined room where now we sat that the clergyman had asked him for a script. A nominal fee—to be paid from the proceeds of the production—all other profits going to replace worm-eaten timbers in the church roof.

Danton Court had stood empty and neglected for twenty years but with the agreement of its trustees the tangled garden could be cleared for spectators. Then, through the gentle deception of concealed lights and evocative voices from the past, the house would live again—its empty rooms ghost-thronged for six short summer nights.

But on the very day Brice completed his script, the bulldozers moved in. No warning. Remote in their London office the trustees forgot that earlier promise. The motorway was coming—and Danton stood in its path. Papers were signed—and the demolition squad arrived.

Still clutching his sheaf of typescript, Timothy Brice had watched a dream vanish in clouds of brickdust.

Now he sat riffling the dog-eared pages as though pained by memories of wasted toil. 'Another victim of progress,' he muttered—and tossed the script into my lap.

'Couldn't you turn it into a book?'

He scowled. 'Nobody *reads*, these days. Anyway, who'd be interested in the history of a place that no longer exists?'

'It's worth a try. If living here has turned you into a peasant, why not move?'

He sank into the deckchair. 'Who'd buy? This place was an RAF transmitter station in the war. Never intended for permanent residence. I took it on as a holiday cottage, years ago. Now? Well—look at it. Neither use nor ornament for a farmer—thanks to that six-lane monstrosity. That's how I managed to get it on the cheap. And somehow I can't see myself living anywhere else.'

'But—your writing. . . .'

He sighed wearily. 'Disappoint you, don't I? But I'm nudging seventy and—to be honest—I don't think I have it in me any more. Not the real thing. If I ever had it at all. You probably think of me as a pretty erudite sort of cove who distilled his historical expertise into drama. The truth is—I'm a sausage machine. Shove in the facts . . . turn the handle—out comes a play. *Grey Walls* was all mugged up from kids' history books. This Danton Court thing . . . I talk about *my* research, but none of it was original. I built with other men's bricks.'

'You knew Hugh Annandale?' I was anxious to get him out of the rut of self-pity.

'Unfortunately, no. Must have been quite a character—especially in his younger days. Towards the end he became something of a recluse—didn't want people prying into his straitened circumstances. Quite a shock for the locals when they turned up for the sale of his furniture and effects. *When they got there, the cupboard was bare.* He must have been stripping the place for years. I suppose you've heard about the wretched way he died.'

'Something. Local opinion points the finger at gypsies. What actually happened?'

'Nobody knows. His housekeeper found the body

on the lawn. He'd been clubbed with the traditional blunt instrument. His old dog had been done in, the same way. Dead for hours. Gypsies? Rubbish. The truth is, nobody wanted to believe a local could have done the dire deed, so . . . it *had* to be an outsider. And whatever they tell you in the village, travelling folk weren't the first suspects. First choice was the airmen, right here in this hut. A rough time they had of it. That I do know, because I've talked to one of them. Ironic—this particular lad was one of the very few people old Annandale took to; the only person who could tell me what life was like at Danton then. I tried old Mrs Thingummy—*Drumsell*—but she wasn't much help. Finding Annandale's body was a great shock for her. She had some kind of breakdown . . . spent a few months in hospital. And she didn't approve of my poking and prying into the past. Told me to leave the dead in peace. Should have taken her advice.'

He was slipping back into despondency. Anne said, 'This airman—how did you contact him?'

'He contacted *me*. On holiday . . . took it into his head to come back for a look at the old place. Sentimental journey. Hadn't been this way for twenty years. Wife . . . kids—a family excursion. After he'd gone I toyed with the idea of writing him into the script. He had quite a story to tell. This hut was practically in a state of siege after old Annandale was killed. Bricks through the windows . . . phone wires cut . . . threats daubed on the walls. Tell me—what's your interest in Danton?'

I told him about the Pompadour Vase and the

reason for our search. He listened intently, leaning forward in the deckchair, hands clasped about his knees. Occasionally he would interrupt, asking me to clarify a detail or expand a point. He found it difficult to understand why Vincent Goring should be so anxious to employ me for a task the police were paid to do.

I explained. 'Fairfield Corporation is going through a difficult time. Last year they were involved in a corruption scandal—something to do with defence contracts. According to Goring they were cleared but he hinted it was a close-run thing and a lot of people weren't happy with the verdict—thought it was a whitewash job. That's had an adverse effect on investment and the possibility of future government contracts. Right now they can't afford trouble of any kind, so you can imagine how they feel about being under surveillance as murder suspects. And even if the police back off, somebody's sure to say it was only because of lack of evidence. That won't help restore Fairfield's tarnished image.'

Brice nodded slowly. 'So all you have to do is find this elusive *Effendi*. You've set yourselves a task, m'dears—and I'm not sure I can help you.' He looked at Anne. 'You were right about those vases. There *are* two. Here, let me have that script. . . .'

He took the sheaf from my hand and skimmed its pages—rapidly at first, then more carefully. 'Ah—here we are. This isn't dialogue, you understand. It's a note for the souvenir programme we planned to sell. I wanted the audience to realise that there was hard fact behind every dramatised episode. There—read it for yourself. The style's contrived—deliberately. Remember, I was trying to describe a piece of rococo extravagance.'

Created over two centuries ago—a royal gift for Madame de Pompadour, its values were manifold. Design, texture and ornament were of an order of artistry such as monarchs may command. But were it possible to gild such excellence, that had been done. The rich madonna-blue, veining its elegance, was compounded from a formula known only to the artist. No such close-guarded secret hid the origin of that bright-gleaming gold which flowed about its contours almost to the point of opulence. That had poured prodigal from the glowing crucible into which had tumbled louis d'or—un-alloyed gold coins of royal France. And the gift had not been limited to this one vase. It had a twin—each peer to other in magnificence.

When Boucher painted a flattering portrait of the Pompadour, there were the vases, artfully placed to flank the couch on which she lay. Another fifty years and they were discovered in an abandoned carriage on a Spanish battlefield during the Peninsular War— fragile survivors from the world before the revolutionary deluge.

The lucky finders—two English cavalry captains, Coote and Annandale—divided their prize in gentlemanly fashion, one vase apiece. Next day a French cannonball lifted Coote's head from his shoulders. It is to Annandale's credit that he personally arranged for Coote's vase to be brought back to his widow in England when he might so easily have appropriated it for his own collection.

I remembered that photograph in Vincent Goring's clenched hand. 'You make it sound as if you'd actually *seen* the Pompadour Vase.'

Brice smiled. 'Other men's bricks—as always. The airman—the one I mentioned—gave me the whole story just as he heard it from old Annandale. And that's all I know.'

I could not hide my disappointment. 'If that vase was sold, Oberon Spreight's talk of theft and skulduggery is rubbish—malicious rubbish.'

The writer scratched his bald head thoughtfully. 'And if the vase was *stolen*, Annandale would have said so when he told Baxter its history. Baxter's the airman. Just remembered his name. I'd say your best bet right now is old Mrs Drumsell. I only hope you get more joy out of her than I did.'

Time to be moving. Outside in the warm sunshine Brice glared angrily at the motorway. 'Look at it—a monument to man's folly. Progress? Come the end of the century it'll be an historic relic—overgrown . . . reverting to nature. Some crank will start a motorway preservation society. That *would* be ironic when you think what they've destroyed to build it. Danton's only part of the story. D'you realise we had a Roman fort, right *there*?' He pointed to where the embankment had smothered acres of rich grazing land. 'And it's not as if nobody knew. But did they bother? Only when the road was less than a mile off. Then—*whoosh*!—archaeologists at it, day and night. Now—*nothing*. Well . . .' He hesitated and eyed me thoughtfully for a moment. 'If I show you something, will you promise not to spread it around?'

He led us to a slab of stone embedded in turf beside the hedge. I stooped to read the inscription, crudely carved but quite legible.

LIVNIVSVIC
TORINVS+FL–
CAELIANVSLEG
AVGLEGVIVICT
PFOBRESTRAIS
VALLVMPRO
SPEREGESTAS

'There!' he exclaimed proudly. 'The tomb of Livnius Victor. That's the only bit I've been able to decipher. I'm no Latinist. Pure luck finding it here. Four feet down, it was. Digging holes is a necessary chore, with no main drainage or refuse collection here. Have to bury everything I can't burn. But when I came across this, and the poor old chap's bones, I filled the hole again and stuck the slab on top. Seemed the right thing to do. Ghoulish—all this grubbing around in graves and shipping bones off to museums. Watched them at it, there in the Roman fort, and I thought *That's not how it's going to be for you, Livnius old sport. You can rest in peace right here.* So—not a word, eh? Leave him alone with his glory.'

At the gate he thrust his script into my hand. 'Read it,' he urged. 'Nobody even bothered to look at it, once the production was scrubbed. It may not be *Grey Walls* but I think it deserves an audience—even an audience of two.'

He stood at the gate watching us walk away. Out on

the far side of the motorway tunnel we looked back. He was still standing there, framed in the archway, his hand raised in farewell.

Anne gripped my hand tightly. 'If I go first,' she said huskily, '*Promise* you won't let yourself get like that.'

I shivered. Colder in that tunnel than I had realised.

CHAPTER
SEVEN

Centuries ago, wayfarers could wade shallow Imber at a ford beside Holy Cross monastery. The village of Croxford grew to house tenant farmers working the wide acres of that religious house. With Dissolution came new landlords and slow plundering of the conventual buildings but memories of poverty, chastity and obedience lingered like fading perfume on the air. The ruined monastery in its sylvan setting inspired Robert Ferrier to build his almshouses for *one dozyn decay'd spynsters*. The institution—*Ferriers Charity*—opened its doors in 1689 and had not lacked a tenant since. Grouped round a court—once the cloister garth—its little redbrick houses remained outwardly unchanged. Here we found Edith Drumsell dozing away that sunny afternoon among rich-scented roses, while urgent bees filled the air with plainsong like echoes from a litany of long-forgotten monks.

'Mr Annandale?' Sleep-blurred eyes fought to focus on my face. 'You know him, sir?'

Polite deference from a woman more than twice my age was disconcerting. I shook my head. 'We were hoping—'

'Does he know you're here?' A bewildered look crept to her face. 'It really is too bad, you know. I can't be expected to do *everything*. Not now.' Agitated waxen fingers clutched the folds of the long black shawl about her shoulders.

Anne leaned forward. 'He knows—but we're not to wait for him. I'm sure you'll be able to help us.'

A soft smile. 'I'll certainly try, madam. What exactly can I do for you?'

Anne fetched a garden chair and sat beside her. 'We'd like to know about the Pompadour Vase.'

'Ah—the *Pompadour*.' The old eyes shone with pride. 'You'll find it in the hall, madam—the alcove at the foot of the stairs.'

'It's still there?' asked Anne. 'We'd heard it was gone.'

Mrs Drumsell frowned. 'Gone? But of course—how silly of me. I forget things, you know. You're quite right, madam—it's down in the cellar. In case of the bombs, you know.'

'It hasn't been sold, then?'

'It's a family *heirloom*, madam.' A touch of *hauteur*. 'One of Mister Hugh's ancestors brought it back from Spain when he was over there with the Duke of Wellington. It's been at Danton ever since, and here it will stay. Master Francis will see to that.'

She was speaking to us from those far-off wartime days before Francis Annandale was killed in action.

'Anybody ever *try* to buy it?' I asked.

A whispered chuckle. 'Oh, they've *tried*, sir—that I know for a fact. But Mr Annandale would no more part with the Pompadour Vase than he'd part with his right arm.'

The shawl slipped as she shifted her position. Carefully, Anne rearranged it about the brittle shoulders. 'Who were they?'

'Ah now that I couldn't say, madam. It's not my place to be concerning myself with Mr Annandale's private business affairs. "Making life easier for you, Drumsell" he'll say. "Another dust-trap gone to a good home". Then I know he's sold some furniture or another ornament. Great one for a joke is Mr Annandale.' The old woman's thin hand reached out to clutch Anne's arm. 'Does he know you're here?'

My wife patted those skeletal fingers reassuringly. 'We'll be going in a minute. So you've no idea who they were?'

The grey head was nodding drowsily. With an effort Edith Drumsell roused herself. 'I'm sorry, madam—what was that?'

Anne looked at me uncomfortably, self-reproach in her eyes. 'It doesn't matter. We won't disturb you any longer.'

Parchment lids drooped over faded blue eyes, but the chatelaine of Danton Court was not yet gone from us. She sighed contentedly and settled deeper into her hair. *'The Fairy King.'* Her voice was little more than a whisper. For a moment I thought that elusive mind had darted back to Victorian childhood.

Anne took one frail relaxed hand as if to summon back departing consciousness. 'Yes?'

'That's what Mr Annandale called him. American. Smoked cigars *with the band on!*' A long pause. 'Wanted *ice* in his whisky.' Silence again, then—with a dying flicker of dignity, *'Not* a gentleman.'

All animation was draining from those ancient features. 'Who was he?' I pleaded urgently. 'Tell us his name.'

But Edith Drumsell had drifted back into dreams more real than wakening.

We stopped the car outside the village, bought a punnet of strawberries from a roadside stall and sat under sun-filtering oaks to enjoy the fresh-picked fruit. In nearby fields gangs of women harvested the succulent pink crop—snatches of conversation and occasional shrieks of laughter reaching us through the hedge.

'*Mmm!*' Anne bit into a strawberry, big as a hen's egg. 'All we need now is Beethoven's *Pastoral*. As a day in the country—perfect; but this surely is no way to run an investigation.'

I flicked a spider-like strawberry stalk into the long grass. 'We know there are two vases.'

'But everything else is guesswork. The Annandale Pompadour was sold some time in the nineteen-forties—*we think*. Effendi just may have bought it—*we think*. Oberon Spreight had a slice of the action—*we think*. Or *you* do.'

'King of the fairies,' I reminded her. 'Midsummer Night's Dream. *Oberon*. Yes?'

She selected another strawberry. 'At the risk of lowering the tone of this conversation—Annandale could have meant something *very* different.'

'I hadn't overlooked that possibility either. *Fairy* had more than one meaning, even in those days, but I can't see a man like Annandale using it to describe a visitor's sexual proclivities. In his army days . . . maybe; at Danton Court—never.'

She grinned. '*Also sprach Zarathustra*. Expert

opinion, professor?'

'Mock me not, woman. I'll have you know I once made a specialised study of graffiti in abandoned military latrines. It's a legitimate subject for research—the flipside of all those true-blue stiff-upper-lip regimental histories. And very revealing.'

'*I'll bet!*'

'I am *trying* to make a serious point. I remember finding the remains of a hutted camp up near the Khyber in Pakistan. Outpost of Empire, don'tcha know. According to British army records, it never existed—yet I was able to date the place, identify the units which used it, in chronological order—even give names and ranks of some of the personnel . . . all from inscriptions scrawled on the lavatory walls. Sure, there's the other side of the picture—the obscenities and the weird poetry—but even that has its interesting points. Do you know, some of the most popular and recurring verses are almost direct translations from Latin originals you can find scratched on Roman latrines from Pompeii to Hadrian's Wall? Which reminds me—Timothy Brice has got himself a very odd inscription.'

Her eyebrows flickered mischievously. 'I didn't notice you taking a peek inside his john.'

'Do not be a twit. I mean that tombstone thing. There's something . . . something *phoney* about it.' I shook my head. 'It's been bothering me ever since he showed it to us. Wish I'd made a copy of the inscription. *Livnius Victor!* Even a kid doing first year Latin would know better than that. It's L Junius Victorinus. Something-or-other. L for Lucius. Can't remember the rest. And it's such a crude bit of work—like a lump of old paving stone. If Brice hadn't found it by accident I'd say someone was putting him on.'

'David.' She patted my knee. 'We are trying to solve a problem in the here and now—remember? Forget your lavatorial graffiti and your Roman tombstones. Concentrate on the matter in hand.'

I concentrated.

After five minutes I said, 'Let's face it—we've turned up nothing worthwhile. What say we drop the whole thing?'

'Seriously? Okay then. At least we've *tried*. Let's get back home . . . have another nice early night . . . maybe drive out and see your folks tomorrow. Or again—maybe not. We could stay in bed till some disgusting hour and then just slop around the place doing nothing in grand style. You look tired, darling. This was supposed to be your vacation but I nagged you into doing that summer school—and look what's happened.' She stood up and held out both hands. 'Come, my lord. I have the medicine shall mend thy melancholy.'

So we drove home to find Dan Peters at our apartment door.

Dying.

He had taken a bullet in the stomach—blood from the wound soaking through his light brown suit and into a raincoat draped over his arm.

In the ambulance he rallied—eyes fluttering open to stare blankly at the white rooflining. I leaned into his line of vision. 'Hang on. We're getting you to hospital.'

Slow recognition crept forward from somewhere far behind his pain-darkened eyes. 'Took your time,' he murmured.

'Don't talk.'

'Must. Listen—he'll try for you next. Has to. Spreight's paying. . . .' The siren blared its fanfare of diminished thirds along Kensington Road. The dying man's lips moved again. *'Effendi,'* he breathed, his eyes pleading with me to understand. Then again, slowly . . . distinctly, *'Effendi.'*

'Sure The name in that letter. I saw it.'

'No. You don't see . . .' The urgency of desperation had crept into his voice. *'Here. . . .'*

'Here? Effendi?'

He nodded weakly. 'Crazy, isn't it?' he said—and died.

While Peters' body was being stripped and examined the uniformed constable who rode in the ambulance interviewed us in an office off the mortuary. Here at least my MOD credentials carried weight. More—he remembered us from five years before when our apartment had been burgled. 'You seem to attract trouble, sir. Didn't I read about you being involved in a spot of bother, couple of years back—up in the Midlands somewhere? Seem to remember something about you being shot on that occasion.'

'An experience I'm anxious not to repeat. You heard Peters tell me this trigger-happy lad with the Turkish nickname is right here in London. I'm next on his list—so we won't be going back to our apartment tonight.'

Anne frowned. 'If there was going to be any trouble, we'd have walked straight into it an hour ago.'

'At the apartment? But Peters was shot somewhere else. You saw the blood he'd leaked on the way in. He must have made a tremendous effort to get to our place and warn us. The man was a pro—he wouldn't lead the opposition straight to our front door. Either he knew he wasn't being followed or he managed to shake off whoever was tailing him. But we're still in danger. Even if Effendi doesn't know our address, he only has to check the phone book.'

'So where does that leave us?' She asked the question quite calmly. We had faced similar situations before.

'Scratching on the Department's door for safe lodging.'

The constable glanced at his notebook. 'This Oberon Spreight character. . . ?'

'The paymaster. That's the way it sounds. Just give me time—I'll find out.'

He looked at me sharply. 'I'll not ask what you mean by that, sir—but let me remind you, this is *our* job.'

My fingers brushed the smear of Peters' blood on my sleeve. 'This makes it *mine*.'

DHR2—oasis of light and activity amidst Whitehall's weekend wilderness of silent offices and deserted corridors, mop-damp and redolent of disinfectant.

There, close on midnight that Saturday, we found Angus Mackintyre laboriously writing up his recent discoveries in Crete. Something in the atmosphere of *DHR2* affects even the most staid members of staff. I had sported a shabby leather-patched cord jacket—mark of my determination not to go native and adopt bowler-hatted regimentals. Angus personified the words of his beloved Burns—*My heart's in the highlands, my heart is not here; My heart's in the highlands a-chasing the deer*—except that he had never chased an animal in his life. Men he would hunt with ruthless determination but when he tramped his northern moors it was to revel in all things living. In Whitehall his tanned face, neat beard and ancient tweeds brought a breath of Scotland, evocative as the reedy lament of bagpipes in a distant glen. If innocent indulgences be counted vices he had but two—whisky and snuff. The former he enjoyed in moderation and never without due ceremony; the latter inordinately from an antique silver snuffbox.

As we entered the office he laid down his pen and regarded us with pleasure unmarked by surprise. 'David . . . Anne—come away in. I was about to brew up, so sit yourselves down and tell me all about it.'

While we talked he busied himself with kettle and teapot—breaking off occasionally to question us on a point in our narrative.

'Yon limb of the law spoke sober truth,' he said, decanting his potent brew into three thick mugs. 'This is police business. You cannot be making it your own personal vendetta, laddie.'

I smiled. 'That's not my intention. This is going to be official.'

He handed me a mug. 'Just how do you intend achieving that?'

I sipped the scalding tea and set it down to cool. 'First step—a formal request for information. That transmitter hut—which airfield was it serving?'

He stood up and crossed to a large wallmap of the British Isles. 'Show me.'

'*There.*'

'Mmm. That would have been Church Orford. Closed for years now. Part of it's a racetrack.'

'We have a file?'

'Unlikely. It was a School of Flying Training. From our point of view, such establishments are usually impeccable.'

'Check it, will you?'

He scratched his beard and regarded me coolly. 'You're officially on leave for another twenty-four hours. Can't it wait till Monday?'

'Time's precious. Once I'm back on duty I'm vulnerable—arriving here each morning . . . leaving each evening. Routine—the hit-man's dream of heaven.'

He stared. 'You'll not nobble this Effendi character within twenty-four hours, I'm thinking—but if it'll bring you peace and contentment I'll away to the morgue.' He drained his mug, noticed Anne's startled expression and patted her arm. '*The muniment room*, lassie.'

He was back in minutes. 'You're in luck, Davie boy. One file, still open. I'll make a bargain. Tell me this is the case you're working on, and I'll make your investigation official.' A broad grin was tugging at his beard.

'Could it have anything to do with Annandale's murder?'

'You're on!' He tossed me the file. *'We know who did it!'*

CHAPTER
EIGHT

In April 1947 five airmen were stationed in that lonely transmitter hut on the edge of Imberbridge. For more than two months their isolation had been aggravated by arctic conditions. Thick snow blanketed Britain. The airfield at Church Orford was out of action—yellow Harvard training aircraft crowded into its vast hangars. With roads impassable to motor traffic, physical communication between airfield and transmitter station depended on men trudging three miles through deep drifts to collect rations and mail. How else they spent their idle days was not recorded in our file. That terse document concentrated on events surrounding the death of Hugh Annandale.

Of the five, four were 'duration of the present emergency' conscripts; one a regular—Michael Power. From County Cork he had crossed the Irish Sea and enlisted in the RAF to avoid a shotgun wedding. Unskilled, he was designated *GD*—General Duties—facing a future of sweeping, cleaning, fetching and carrying. He speedily earned a reputation for trouble-making and what his superiors chose to call *dumb insolence*. Posting to that remote transmitter hut was the nearest the Air Force could come to banishment. The inhabitants from Imberbridge took no such detached view. Ugly scenes at the *Dun Cow* culminated in Power's involuntary exit, horizontal—

an attitude he maintained, three feet above the ground, for several yards. Caught stealing eggs, he was soundly thrashed by an irate farmer. Two nights later the farmer's haystacks were fired. Because snowdrifts kept the fire brigade away from Imberbridge, flames engulfed a nearby barn. Nothing was proved but local anger began to simmer dangerously.

Then, when Spring had finally come, Power was found one night, prowling about Danton Court. Hugh Annandale set a dog on him but he escaped into the dusk, leaving threats of retribution upon the darkening air. The police were notified and next evening a local sergeant cycled to Church Orford and obtained the Commanding Officer's promise that Air Force discipline would dampen the fiery Irishman's ardour.

But by dawn Hugh Annandale was dead and Michael Power gone—none knew whither. He had boasted of money, proudly flashing five-pound notes at a time when the crisp white fiver was a rarity. The official view was that he had returned across the Irish border. Well rid of him, the RAF made no attempt to trace the path of his flight, preferring to leave that to the civil police. But for thirty years a file had remained open. . . .

All of which made fascinating reading but my interest lay with 2329880 AC2 Baxter, R.P.—the man Annandale befriended. Released from service, January 5 1949—London address. Recall for duty—Suez crisis 1956—deferred. Registered college student 1953–57. Last known address—The School House, East Tupton near Newark in Nottinghamshire—1965. RAF Records were no longer interested but *DHR2* keeps tabs on everyone concerned with an open file. I checked the latest phone directory. He was still in his school house.

'I need wheels.'

Angus shook his head. 'You need sleep, laddie. It's past two. Baxter won't thank you for disturbing him at some ungodly hour on the Sabbath. Bide here, the pair of you. Kip in the duty officer's bunk and set off fresh as paint, the morn.'

He spoke with the subtle insistence of an hypnotist. My lids began to droop. I blinked. 'And then we find Baxter's out for the day.'

Anne smothered a yawn. 'Why's he so important? If the Pompadour Vase was sold before he knew Hugh Annandale. . . .'

'But was it? That description in Brice's script—'

'You think Baxter actually *saw* the vase? The old man could have told him . . . shown him a picture. David, you're clutching at straws.'

'There's nothing else. Look—out there is a man with a gun. He's killed Peters . . . most likely killed Kendrick and that other poor devil who helped him. I'm next in line. Why? *Because he thinks I'll identify him*. Don't you see what that means?'

Angus tugged his beard thoughtfully. 'Aye—it means there's a clue somewhere; something you're capable of working out. You should find that very encouraging, Davie.' He pinched the tip of his nose. '*Effendi*. Turkish, isn't it? The respectful way to address a government official. Have you not tried working along that line?'

'Give me time.' I thumped my fist against the table. 'It *has* to be connected with Danton. Baxter's our only lead—but he won't lead anywhere while we sit here. Come on, Angus—scrawl your name on a little green chitty and release us one authorised vehicle, staff for the use of.'

'Man, you're in no fit state—' He saw my expression. 'All right, all right. Since you're set on this folly, here's what I'll do. I'll drive you myself. I had me a wee nap earlier, so I'll not be falling asleep at the wheel.' He waved his snuffbox magisterially. 'Hoity-toity—no use looking down your nose, laddie. This is how it has to be. Man, you know I'm the last person to insist on protocol but we could be in big trouble if I let you go ahead on your own. Think how it would look— a Grade Three investigation initiated by the head of another department still officially on leave—while I sit here twiddling my thumbs. Heads would indubitably roll. And if things go wrong—I mean *really* wrong— have you thought about that? I stand by my bargain, but we do things by the book.'

He took a huge pinch of snuff and brushed his moustache with a red-patterned handkerchief. Ten minutes later we were down in the basement where he garaged his personal transport—a diminutive puce-coloured saloon.

'But . . . it's a kiddie-car,' protested Anne from the rear seat.

'Half-price motoring, lassie.' Angus settled himself behind the wheel. 'Seventy miles to the gallon—think of that. When your President gets to driving one of these I'll know he's taking the energy crisis seriously.'

We shot out of the garage, speeding through near-deserted streets to join the highway they used to call The Great North Road.

'And another thing—' Angus broke in on our thoughts to enthuse further over his tiny vehicle. 'I pay less than half the road tax you do.'

'Mmm?' Anne was already dozing. 'How come?'

'This little beauty's classed as a tricycle.'

I stared at him. 'A *what*?'

His grinning face was silhouetted against the street lights. 'Had you not noticed? You asked for wheels, laddie—but you didn't specify how many. We're travelling on three. Relax.'

From where the River Trent flows beneath the walls of Newark Castle fifteen miles stretch northwards to East Tupton—a straggling village dominated by the spire of its vast church.

We found Baxter's house beside the mid-Victorian school—both buildings reflecting the gothic tastes of that period. Though the school had been modernised and enlarged, the house retained its original appearance—grey stone walls, mullioned windows, diamond leaded panes. Impressive.

Closed curtains suggested our pedagogue was abed. We roused him.

He stood at the door, blinking in the early sun—tall . . . fifty . . . slight academic stoop. Wisps of grey flecked the thick brown hair but his face had retained the openness of youth—a kind of profound innocence, wise yet eager to learn more. He made no protest at being disturbed while the village slept.

'Ministry of Defence? That has an ominous ring about it. Make yourselves comfortable while I get some clothes on.'

We waited in his study, a scholar's room—book-lined and hung with pictures of ancient buildings, mostly Greek and Roman. On his desk stood a red Samian-ware bowl in process of restoration, fragments of its shattered rim still awaiting the delicate attention of his skilled hands. Above one bookcase hung a racing scull inscribed with the names of a college eight in which R P Baxter had rowed, twenty-five years before.

He was back, hastily clad in blue shirt, jeans and sandals. 'Now,' he said as we sank into comfortable armchairs, 'what's it all about? Must be urgent to bring you hotfoot from London at this unseemly hour.'

I glanced at the official file. 'You were Aircraftsman Robert Peter Baxter?'

His eyes widened in amused surprise. 'That's ancient history. What is this—a court-martial?'

'We're enquiring into circumstances surrounding the death of Hugh Annandale. You were—'

'Hold on!' He put a hand to his head. 'Let me get this straight. You're enquiring into poor old Annandale's death *now*—after thirty years?'

'It's our job. As it happens, I'm an archaeologist—'

He roared with laughter. 'You need to be if you're investigating *that* case. This is ludicrous!'

Angus frowned. 'No laughing matter, Mr Baxter. We need information. A man's life may depend on it.'

Immediately he was serious. 'Paddy Power? Don't

tell me you've caught up with him after all this time.'

'You think he was guilty?' I asked.

His brows lifted. 'What I think is no concern of yours. With respect, I fail to see why the Ministry of Defence is investigating the murder of a civilian. Surely that's a job for the police.'

I put up a hand to stem his rising indignation. 'I withdraw the question. Let's not get off on the wrong foot. When Mr Mackintyre spoke of a man's life being in danger, he meant me. As far as I'm concerned the guilt or innocence of Michael Power is of only minor importance. I'm far more interested in Hugh Annandale and what you may or may not have seen when you visited Danton Court. Yesterday we talked with Timothy Brice the playwright. He says you once told him about a vase—the Pompadour Vase. Did you ever *see* it?'

The question clearly surprised him but he replied without hesitation. 'Of course. Lovely thing. He had it stowed away in a trunk, all padded round with pillows.'

'*When* did you see it?'

'Heavens! You don't expect the exact date, surely? Early forty-seven some time. The old boy was in an expansive mood—chuntering on about the treasures he'd been forced to sell. Took me down to the cellar and showed me the vase. Had his old army uniform down there too. Did you know he fought at the battle of Omdurman?'

I remembered that letter with its reference to *the old British scarlet*. 'Did he let you try it on?'

Baxter shook his head. 'Wouldn't have fitted me. Old Annandale was slightly built. Not much above five feet eight, I'd say.'

Angus was fingering his snuffbox. 'This vase now— did you tell anyone about it?'

'May have done. Annandale hadn't sworn me to secrecy or anything dramatic like that—though I should think the thing was pretty valuable.'

'You can say that again,' murmured Anne.

Angus glared at her. 'Could it be that you told Michael Power?' he persisted.

The teacher's shoulders flexed in a brief shrug. 'Shouldn't think so. A good sort, old Paddy, but no interest in the finer things of life. Still . . . if I did mention it, he'd have heard. Privacy was a luxury denied us in that hut. Five men living in each other's laps. The joys of service life!'

Angus took a pinch of snuff, plied his handkerchief and turned to me. 'Motive for murder, Davie? Power hears about the vase, steals it—but meets up with Annandale in the process.'

Baxter's knuckles whitened as he gripped the arms of his chair and leaned forward. 'You can rule out Paddy Power. For one thing, the Pompadour Vase wasn't . . . well—like *that*.' He indicated the Samian pot on his desk. 'You'd need a padded crate—hell of a job for one man to carry. Besides—Paddy wasn't the villain people seemed to think.'

'He threatened Annandale,' I said.

'Threatened?' He frowned. 'Oh—*that*. When old Annandale set his dog on him. I'm not surprised—but whatever he's supposed to have said, he wouldn't *mean* it. Not old Paddy. A big mouth—that was his trouble. Get a few pints inside him and he was insufferable. But never violent. No—all those smug self-righteous people, so quick to point the finger at him—*they* were the ones for violence. Worked him over in the pub one night. Chucked him out. I mean literally *chucked*. You should have seen him when he got back to the hut. He was in a *state*. And another time one of the local farmers beat him up.'

'For stealing eggs.'

'Got a record of that too, have you? My God—Paddy was right when he said the Air Force had it in for him. Eggs? What the hell would we want eggs for? Five of us in that hut, but they kept sending rations for eight. Eggs? We were sick of the sight of them! No—if you ask me that farmer was just carrying on where they left off in the *Dun Cow*. And that was all over nothing.'

I tapped the file. 'Arson? Haystacks . . . a barn . . .'

'For heaven's sake! Who's been feeding you all this guff? Listen—when Paddy got back after that little episode with Farmer Giles he was in bed for two days. I tell you—he was in a bad way. Yet he's supposed to have got up . . . ploughed through waist-high snow-drifts . . . fired a haystack—and got back without us knowing.'

'You knew he had an alibi? Why didn't you speak up?'

'Because he asked us not to. He wasn't being charged. All that talk about arson was just malicious gossip. What bothered him was the risk of getting more black marks on his service record. If we'd said he was in bed when he should have been on duty, they'd have nailed him for not reporting sick—and if the truth came out, they'd take the farmer's word against his.'

'So why did he up and run?' demanded Angus.

Another shrug. 'He'd had enough. Annandale had lodged a complaint about him snooping round Danton Court. That meant more trouble—maybe more rough justice from the delightful citizens of Imberbridge. So he upped and went.'

'He had money,' I said. 'A lot.'

'Is that so?' Baxter's level gaze met mine.

I asked about Effendi but the name meant nothing. Annandale preferred formality in the matter of names. He had never addressed Baxter by his Christian name. As their friendship developed he became *Baxter*—never *Robert*. The old man shrank from anything approaching affection, though he made liberal use of nicknames.

I glanced at Angus and read disappointment in his eyes. What had our journey achieved? Nothing but the knowledge that the Pompadour Vase, still at Danton Court within weeks of Annandale's death, had disappeared by the time his effects were sold. I questioned Baxter about that sale, asking if he had not been surprised that the vase was not included.

'I wasn't around. Things got rough after the murder. That little hut's very vulnerable, stuck in the middle of a field. They damn near got to us more than once—those stalwart sons of toil from charming Imberbridge. The Air Force pulled us back to main camp and then posted us off to other stations. I didn't see the old place again for more than twenty years. We were on our way to Stratford and I made a detour— the time we met Timothy Brice. How is the old chap? Still scribbling?'

'He's a sad old man,' said Anne. 'That motorway just about destroyed him.'

'Motorway?'

'Danton Court stood right in its path. They started demolition the very day he finished his script about it.'

Baxter whistled. 'That must have been a blow. He had great hopes of that production. Small beer after the stuff he was turning out thirty years ago, but it was going to let people know Timothy Brice wasn't over the hill.'

'He's way over, now,' said Anne sadly. 'Or the hill's over him. The embankment is only a few yards from the hut. Completely smothered a Roman fort. Did you know about that?'

'I knew there was a Roman site there. Did they manage to excavate? I reckon to hear about most emergency digs but I missed that one.'

'They mounted some sort of rescue operation,' I told him. 'Brice says everyone was caught on the hop.'

'I'll bet. Don't suppose anyone in Imberbridge even knew it was there. But I'm surprised old Brice hadn't done anything about having it excavated. Right up his street.'

I shook my head. 'He's a romantic. Real down-to-earth archaeology's not his scene. Accidentally dug up a Roman tombstone—but instead of excavating, he developed a conscience about disturbing the dead. Doesn't even know Latin. Amazing—he writes about the Romans but can't translate a simple Latin inscription.' I chuckled. '*Livnius Victor!*'

'Come again?'

'He thought he'd found the tomb of someone called Livnius Victor. I hadn't the heart to tell him the name was Lucius Junius Victorinus.'

Anne smiled. 'I'm afraid David's idol had feet of clay.'

Baxter appeared not to have heard her. 'This tombstone,' he said. 'What's it like?'

I spread my hands. 'About *so* big. Brice thinks it's genuine but I'm not convinced. Wish I'd examined it more closely—not that it has anything to do with our investigation.'

Leaning sideways he ran his hand along the serried volumes and twitched a slim brown book from the shelf. He turned its pages rapidly . . . paused . . . flicked a few more sheets and then, with a grunt of satisfaction, held it out for us to see. 'This?'

We were looking at a neatly-drawn sketch of a Roman relic—a stone slab on which an inscription had been carved.

LIVNIVSVIC
TORINVS + FL

I stared at him. 'The words, yes—but the stone was different. More like—'

'—a broken paving slab?' he suggested. 'Because that's what it was. And I'm damned if I know what it's doing at Imberbridge. Paddy Power sold it.' He threw back his head and roared with mirth. 'Sold it for fifty quid. To a Yank.'

CHAPTER
NINE

With Baxter's yellow Datsun on its tail the three-wheeler took two and a half hours to reach Imber-bridge. Each time Angus encountered a vehicle similar to his own he would celebrate the event with flashing headlights and exaggerated salutes—a form of amiable lunacy apparently common among the tricycling fraternity. As we squeezed from the close-confining fibreglass shell to join Baxter at Brice's gate, the peace of the countryside surged round us. Mingled with birdsong came a distant peal of churchbells. Only the endless motorway traffic struck an alien note. A convoy of easyrider motorcyclists moved along the skyline like ducks in a fairground shooting-gallery—the hornet whine of their twostroke engines strident on the breeze.

Timothy Brice, emerging from the old transmitter hut belligerent as a stag at bay, relaxed as he recognised Anne, Baxter and myself. But he clearly regarded Angus with suspicion. I explained our purpose.

'*Open the grave?*' He was incredulous. 'That's exactly what I've been trying to avoid. You disappoint me, Doctor Meynell. I particularly asked you not to mention that tombstone.'

Baxter opened his little brown book. 'Take a look at that.'

Brice studied the picture then stumped to the hedge and stood comparing sketch and stone slab. 'I don't get it,' he said.

Baxter joined him. 'That's Collingwood Bruce's *Handbook to the Roman Wall*. Had it with me when I was stationed here. That hard winter, the problem was knowing how to pass the time. Cards . . . books . . . radio. I hit on the idea of making my own Roman relic. Copied this one. It's an altar not a tombstone. Dedicated by Lucius Junius Victorinus Flávius Caelianus, commander of the Victorious, Pious and Faithful Sixth Legion, on account of successful operations north of the Wall. If you'd read it thoroughly, Doctor Meynell, you'd have realised it doesn't belong here. The original was found up at Kirksteads by Hadrian's Wall.'

'A forgery!' bellowed Brice. 'A cheap hoax!'

'Nothing of the sort,' said Baxter calmly. 'I wasn't out to deceive anyone. It was just something to do. The only tools I had were a hammer and a few six-inch nails. I mean—*look* at the thing! It wouldn't deceive a child.' He coughed, realising what he had said. 'Obviously if you found the thing four feet down, you'd naturally think—'

Brice glared at the slab. 'Why bury the damn thing in the first place?' he demanded.

'I didn't.' Baxter gazed slowly round the field as if measuring distance. 'You found it here—right *here* on this very spot?'

'Correct. I was going to bury some rubbish.'

The schoolteacher snapped his fingers excitedly. '*Rubbish!*'

'Eh?' Brice was still seething.

'It's all coming back to me now. Every week a truck used to come out from main camp. Job for the German prisoners of war. There were still some around, even then. They used to empty our dustbins and the chemical toilet. Funny little truck it was, with small wheels. We used to call it—' He glanced at Anne. 'Well, never mind what we used to call it. The point is, when the snow came it got bogged down. Couldn't make the trip. We had to bury everything. Most of the time we were living out of cans. Tinned meat . . . tinned vegetables . . . tinned fruit. Even the cheese came in big cans. The empties began to mount up. Digging holes was no joke with the ground frozen solid, so we packed it in. Used to stand at the door with a pile of empty cans and see who could throw furthest. They'd go sailing off and—*plop*!—into the snow. Out of sight . . . out of mind—until the thaw! When the snow melted, what did we see? Ever-decreasing semi-circles of rusty cans radiating from the door. Not a pretty sight—and of course, the signals officer *had* to arrive for a snap inspection before we'd got the place tidied up. He was not amused, believe you me. Ordered us to dig a damn great pit and bury the stuff—but insisted it be left open for inspection the following week. We went down at least six feet but by the time he arrived it was full of water. After the snow . . . floods—remember? So then he cursed us for leaving an open pit full of water. Death-trap, he called it.'

'And that's not just a figure of speech,' I said grimly, turning to Brice. '*Bones*, you said.'

The writer nodded. 'A human skeleton—and don't

tell me that's a forgery too.' He glanced at Baxter. 'You still haven't explained how your handiwork came to be down there.'

'I can't. It's a mystery to me. When I'd finished chipping away at that old bit of paving stone I set it up outside the hut. Something else the signals officer didn't take kindly to when he came snooping around. Told me to lose it. Wasn't going to have his transmitter station turned into a museum. I was all set to chuck it down the hole along with the rubbish when, *bingo!*—it vanished. Next thing I knew, Paddy Power was waving fivers under my nose. He'd flogged it to an American. Offered me a fiver—which I was sorely tempted to accept—and asked me how many more relics I could knock out in the next week.' He shook his head. 'None of which explains what it was doing down there in our rubbish tip—with a skeleton for company.'

I looked at my watch. 'Time's ticking on. Mr Brice—your spade!'

It took half an hour to find the skeleton. Urgent though our task was, we observed the rudiments of archaeology, checking every spadeful of earth for supportive evidence. Six beer bottles and two *Brylcreem* jars. Then Angus Mackintyre was down in the pit, stooping over a dirt-encrusted tibia which thrust from the soil like an admonishing yellow finger.

'Hmm.' He stroked his beard and darted an accusing glare at Brice. 'No doubt you disturbed things, poking about.' His Scottish brogue had become more pronounced—sure sign he was engrossed in his work.

The writer bridled. 'I did not *poke about*,' he protested hotly. 'As soon as I realised what I'd found I left well alone. True, some of the bones may have been slightly disturbed, but—'

'No matter.' Angus cut him short. 'Where was the stone?'

'Down there—about four feet.'

Angus took a deep breath. 'Man, I *know* it was down here. Where in relation to the body? On top? Underneath? To one side?'

Brice hesitated. 'To one side . . . I *think*. I came across it first—before I found the bones.' He drew himself up haughtily. 'You must understand, sir—I did not regard myself as an archaeologist recording the exact location of my discovery for the benefit of posterity.'

Ignoring this, Angus spoke to Baxter who had stripped to the waist and was leaning patiently on a spade. 'Start clearing along thataway. Gently now . . . gently. I want a record of every stage.' He snatched a Polaroid instant camera from the litter of equipment by his feet and aimed it at the leg bone. 'What we need now is dustpan and brush. Mr Brice—?' He turned hopefully but Timothy Brice was striding angrily towards the hut.

Anne shook her head—a mother wearied by petulant children. 'Angus, you really are hopeless. He's not one of your staff to be bullied and ordered around.' She sighed. 'Leave it to me. I'll sort things out.' She hurried after the outraged playwright.

Angus stared in genuine bewilderment. 'What have I done now?'

'*Hey!*' Baxter's excited cry drew attention back to the pit. He had uncovered the upper part of the skeleton and was pointing to a small object, lodged near the skull. 'I recognise this. It's Paddy Power's crucifix.'

Angus snorted professional scepticism. 'Millions of crucifixes in the world and you're sure *that* belonged to Power. Got his name on it?'

'As good as.' Baxter held out the tiny object. 'Carved it himself from a piece of perspex—you know, the plastic glass they used in aircraft.' He looked down at the tumbled skeleton. 'That's Paddy all right.'

But Angus was not convinced. 'Be logical, man. You told us he sold your spurious relic for fifty pounds. What's to say he didn't sell this too? Passed it off as a genuine Celtic artifact. That way, it doesn't have to be Power down there.'

The schoolteacher was unperturbed. 'He wouldn't sell this. Had it blessed by the chaplain—so that put it beyond price in Paddy's eyes. Look—I *knew* the man. You didn't.'

Anne was back with dustpan, brush and a broken dinner knife. 'He's fixing us a meal,' she said, nodding towards the hut. 'No thanks to Angus.'

She handed the tools to Baxter who resumed work around the skeleton, kneeling beside it and plying knife and brush with obvious skill.

'You've done this sort of thing before,' I said admiringly, watching him probe and scrape with surgical precision. He paused, eased back onto his haunches and for some moments stayed there, staring down.

Then he slowly turned his head and looked up at me over his shoulder—disquiet on his sweat-streaked face.

'What are we getting into?' he asked huskily—and pointed to the object at his feet.

Another skull.

Brice had set chairs round a couple of card-tables in the largest room of his ramshackle home. Thirty years before it had housed the softly-humming transmitters on which trainee pilots depended from the moment they were strapped in their cockpits.

Sadly our host's hospitality outstripped his culinary skill. I had looked forward to homegrown salad . . . eggs . . . goat's milk. Instead he chose to assault our palates with canned gunge. Glutinous gobbets of meat-flavoured soya flour swam before us in thick brown gravy where anonymous vegetable-matter struggled like Bunyan's Pilgrim in the Slough of Despond. Slurping our way through that ill-conceived stew we reviewed facts.

'Forensic science is not my scene,' admitted Angus, unashamedly picking his teeth with a sharpened matchstick. 'If there's any evidence to say how Power died, I haven't seen it. But I'd hazard more than a guess the other fellow was battered to death. Did you not see how the front of the skull was smashed in? Takes a lot of force to do that kind of damage. Going by the way the bone's splintered, his own mother wouldn't have recognised him.'

Baxter regarded his plate with ill-concealed loath-ing. 'The damage could have been inflicted after death—to make him unrecognisable. Either way, I don't believe Paddy Power was responsible.' He set his knife and fork together and leaned back with a sigh of relief. 'What sort of crazy scenario are we supposed to imagine? Say Paddy was telling the truth—that he'd sold my stone to an American. What's it doing back here?'

Anne sipped a glass of water. '*Caveat emptor*. Maybe the buyer realised he'd been swindled and came back for his money. They quarrel . . . the American gets his head smashed but grabs Paddy and in they go—still clutching the stone.'

'No chance. Four feet of water—that's all there was after we'd dumped our rubbish—and Paddy a six-footer? He'd have scrambled out in half a minute. And when's this supposed to have happened? None of us in here heard a thing.'

She toyed with her glass. 'Was Paddy with you, the second time your officer came?'

Baxter nodded. 'We were all on parade. But that night Paddy disappeared. We filled in the hole next day.'

Her eyes widened. 'Didn't it occur to you that he might have fallen in?'

'Frankly no. Wasn't the first time he'd slipped away for a night. We were a law unto ourselves, out here. As long as a man did his fair whack, nobody enquired too closely about his spare-time activities. Paddy reckoned himself a bit of a stud. Need I say more?'

Angus wiped his matchstick and slipped it back in a Swan Vestas box. 'You posit the existence of a third party?' he queried.

Baxter smiled at the pedantic tone. 'I do?'

'Surely—if you dismiss the idea of a violent quarrel on the brink of that pit, someone else disposed of Power and this other fellow.'

'*Fellow?*' demanded Anne. 'What if the second skeleton's a girl? That makes sense. Paddy Power the Imberbridge Stud . . . outraged husband or boyfriend catches him fooling around.'

I smiled. 'And the stone slab? Your theory only works if the outraged gent was the American—who just happened to be toting that twenty-pound chunk of masonry when he caught up with the star-crossed lovers.'

Angus glowered at us. 'Have you two finished concocting your romantic fantasy? We've got ourselves two *male* skeletons. You doubt that—after seeing those pelvic cavities? Heavens—if you missed *that*, is it worth asking if you noticed anything strange about the second skeleton?'

I pictured the scene when Baxter finished clearing earth from the bones. One of those bodies had lain for thirty years as if asleep—outstretched, with knees slightly bent. The other. . . .

'Oddly positioned?' I suggested cautiously.

He turned away in disgust. 'That the sort of nebulous jargon you put in your field reports? Man—it was all of a heap! Everything higgledy-piggledy. He dragged a wad of Polaroid prints from his pocket, shuffled them and dealt me a picture. 'See? What *was* yon poor wee fellow—a contortionist who died in the middle of his act? Either those bones were disturbed a long time after death—'

'Which they were *not*!' muttered Brice, returning an accusing glare.

'—or the body was dismembered and thrown into that pit piecemeal.' Angus snapped open his snuffbox and lifted a pinch of pungent brown powder towards his nose. With finger and thumb level with his chin he hesitated. 'But . . . if *that's* the case—where's the evidence to support it? No sawcuts . . . no splintering at the joints. . . .'

'There are signs of damage,' Baxter reminded him helpfully.

With two loud sniffs Angus inhaled the mentholated tobacco. 'Aye—skull, ribcage and collarbone. But not consistent with post-mortem dissection.' He rubbed his hands together briskly. 'An intriguing problem.'

Anne laid a hand on my sleeve. 'This third person—could it be the one we're after?'

I pondered. 'Let's just check what we've *got* against what we *want*. Assume there was a third party. He—she?—was here in Imberbridge at the time Annandale was murdered and Paddy Power disappeared. That's within the period the Pompadour Vase dropped out of sight. Three dead bodies and a possible connection with the vase. Now—thirty years on—we have three more bodies, Matt Kendrick, Ollie Piper and Dan Peters, connected with that same vase.'

Angus flung up despairing hands. 'The good Lord preserve us from such blatantly un— . . . un— . . . *aaah*—' Violent sneezes shook his whole body. 'unscientific reasoning.'

I ignored him and turned to Baxter. 'How did

Power meet up with the American?'

'He never told me. I've always assumed it was one
of the army types around at the time. Couple of them
called here in a jeep. Wanted to know if they were
right for Imberbridge. Weren't many signposts in
those days. Medical chaps by the look of them. Saw
them buzzing about once or twice after that. One—ah
a *very* exalted gent. Colonel or some such—never
could work out their badges of rank. Called me *soldier*
all the time. And decorations! Fruit-salad all over his
chest.'

'No idea what they were doing here?'

'Haven't a clue. But they left in style. Quite a pro-
cession along the road out there. Military police—you
know, white helmets and those big Harley-Davidson
bikes—a jeep, a staff-car . . . and an ambulance.' He
looked at our host. 'You're the Imberbridge his-
torian—any idea what it was all about?'

Brice frowned. 'An *ambulance*? Obviously somebody ill or injured. Somebody important, to judge
from that impressive *entourage*. A high-ranking
officer. *Hmm*. That rings a bell. But no—that was a
few years earlier. Yes, that was during the war.' Without another word he stood up and shuffled from the
room. As on the previous day, muffled thuds and
crashes from along the corridor—Brice among his
archives. He returned brandishing a close-printed
press cutting. 'Toyed with the idea of putting this in
my script but it's hardly a significant chapter in the
history of Danton Court.'

*   *   *

General Cyrus Brandon was a man in a hurry. His journey from Sicily, plagued by misfortunes and changes of plan, had included an overlong flight in a British Sunderland. The grey flying-boat had climbed aloft from Gibraltar's troubled waters where just three weeks earlier a RAF Liberator carrying another general—the Polish Wladyslaw Sikorski—had plunged into the sea. At 5,000 feet the Sunderland turned west, making a wide sweep out over the Atlantic to avoid Focke-Wulf patrols around the Bay of Biscay. Hours of watching the wrinkled ocean crawl beneath the great aircraft's floats put increased strain on Brandon's already overtaxed patience. Due at a vital planning conference in Hampshire at 10.00 on July 27, he chafed at this leisurely detour. For five hours the four Pratt and Witney Wasps dragged their payload northwest at 200mph. At 18.30 on July 26 the pilot swung the Sunderland onto a bearing which would bring it eastwards to Southampton Water. Almost immediately his radio operator passed him a message ordering a diversion due to enemy action over the English Channel.

So it was that in the dusk of that day General Brandon was ferried ashore—fuming with impatience—to find himself in Belfast, four hundred miles from his destination. Urgent signals brought a US Army Piper Cub light aircraft to the nearest airstrip at dawn. With the general aboard it took off again at 0430 heading east across the Mull of Galloway and the Solway Firth to put down for fuel near Carlisle. From there its course lay south-south-east, following the Pennine Chain, England's geological vertebrae—over

*open moorland and across the industrial conurbations
of Yorkshire and the North Midlands. Around Not-
tingham the plane hit strong headwinds—outriders of a
severe storm coming up from the south. For twenty
minutes the tiny Piper was buffetted among ever-
thickening clouds, its speed reduced to 60mph. With
fuel low, the pilot abandoned the flightplan which
would have put them down on a USAAF strip.
Through broken cloud he glimpsed runways below.
His chart identified Church Orford—confirmed by
Traffic Control at Orford Tower who cleared him to
land. He swung the Piper in a wide circle and began his
approach from the north. Two miles from the runway
the light aircraft plunged into torrential rain. At that
critical moment visibility was suddenly restricted to
twenty yards. The pilot found himself over an unfamiliar runway at 150 feet. Playing safe, he opened the
throttle intending to climb and circle again but gusting
wind caught the Piper under its starboard wing, thwart-
ing its struggle to gain precious altitude.*

*At less than 100 feet it roared over olive-green fields
of rain-flattened barley to skim the roof of Danton
Court.*

*Directly ahead lay the transmitter hut and—thrusting
upwards from the field beside it—a newly-erected VHF
aerial.*

*The port wing clipped that wire-braced steel pole,
sending the Piper spinning like a boomerang back
towards Danton.*

*It crashed into a cluster of tall horse-chestnuts and
fell noisily to the ground—a tangled butterfly dying
amid showers of raindrops and splintered wood.*

Three days later General Cyrus Brandon was buried with full military honours in Imberbridge church-yard.

CHAPTER
TEN

The newspaper version on which that account is based was in a style beloved of wartime newsreel commentators. Clichés abounded, descriptions were laboured, adjectives overworked. The Piper Cub's pilot was invariably *intrepid*, his passenger by turns *determined*, *resolute* or *indomitable*. I could picture a well-thumbed copy of Roget's *Thesaurus of English Words and Phrases* propped beside the journalist's typewriter. Yet the story got across—in great detail.

When Timothy Brice finished reading there was a long silence. In the distance a motorcycle sped east along the motorway—its engine a fresh-awakened echo of that doomed aircraft.

'When was that written?' I asked.

He shrugged. 'It's headed *WARTIME TRAGEDY RECALLED*. Hang about though. Hang a-*bout*. Bit here in the next column "*These wartime events are being recalled in Imberbridge with the news that General Brandon's remains are about to be exhumed for reburial in his family vault in America. We are indebted to Mr H. Annandale of Danton court for . . .*" The rest is missing.'

'I guess Hugh Annandale supplied the details,' suggested Anne. 'It happened right on his doorstep.'

I fished for my glasses. 'Let's see that.'

The reverse side was part of a report headed *NEWS*

FROM THE WOMEN'S INSTITUTES listing varied activities from the previous month—March. A catalogue of woe. The speaker invited to address Matley Institute had failed to arrive. Only four members had attended the meeting at Caveden. For the third month in succession ladies of the Dunwell Institute—or seven of their number—had foregathered in the Vicarage (by kind invitation of Mrs Prentice) because the village hall was still without electricity. For all these misfortunes—and more—there was but one reason.

I read the report to the others. '*Thick snow*. Must have been nineteen forty-seven.'

Angus took another pinch of snuff. 'Or fifty-three. That was a hard winter.'

'Not with Hugh Annandale still around. It *has* to be forty-seven. That military convoy would be General Brandon's funeral cortege—second time round. The army doesn't go in for hearses, so they'd stick the coffin in an ambulance. Police escort . . . medical team to supervise the exhumation . . . it all fits. But—if one of them went missing. . .?' I stared at Angus.

As if reading my thoughts he said quietly, 'Aye—not a pretty picture is it, Davie?'

A puzzled frown creased Baxter's forehead. 'You've lost me.'

Angus blew a trumpet-blast into his handkerchief. 'Simple logic,' he muttered. 'Two skeletons—right? One almost certainly Michael Power. The other? If it was one of the medical team detailed to exhume General Brandon's body there'd be one hell of a fuss when he went missing. The team wouldn't just drive off the way they did. And here's another thought. You saw that contingent leave. Was that before or after Annandale was killed?'

'After. We got the news about Annandale when the police came here to the hut. That was early in the morning. I saw the Americans leaving soon after.'

'Right when the police were hunting a killer. If one of those GIs had disappeared overnight, d'you think the others would have been allowed to drive off like that? So obviously they were up to full strength. Yet we have *two* skeletons.' He shuffled his wad of Polaroid prints. 'Take a look at the second one again. Extensive damage to the frontal structure. Damage? *Extensive* damage? Yes? Oh come on, man—it's obvious!' He brought the outstretched fingers of his right hand against the palm of his left in a slow miming action. '*Zeeow! Poom!*'

Baxter stared incredulously. 'The plane crash? *Brandon?*'

Westminster chimes drifted along Whitehall and in at the office window. Six o'clock. I dug a battery shaver from my desk, whirred away the stubble and strode smooth-jowled down shadowy corridors.

Summoned from Sunday golf the Director sat in his quiet room studying a chessboard where stood seven red and five white pieces—unmoved since his opponent, KGB Colonel Arnov, disappeared from the Kremlin three months before. He did not look up as I entered but after a few moments he sniffed suspiciously. 'Enlighten me. *What* is that pungent aroma about your person? Our late colleague Metcalfe would doubtless have described it as reminiscent of an Alexandrian knocking-shop.'

I resented the casual reference to Ron Metcalfe—two years in his grave. 'Pre-shave,' I said curtly.

'Indeed? When I was your age, dear boy, it was not considered necessary to advertise the deployment of one's razor with quite such ostentation. But—to business. Mackintyre has told me the gist of your remarkable theory. Pray elaborate.'

I settled in one of the green leather club chairs. 'Baxter—the schoolteacher from East Tupton—gave me the idea. He said anyone who took the Pompadour Vase would need a padded crate. What happened when they exhumed General Brandon's body? From my experience, they'd stow the remains in a bag and transfer them to a new coffin. And what *is* a coffin? It's a padded crate. Now the Pompadour Vase disappeared from Danton Court about that time and eventually reappeared in America. What better way of shipping a valuable antique—for which the police would be searching—than in the funeral casket of a three-star general?'

The Director leaned forward to snap flame from a silvered handgrenade on his desk. 'And at the other end?' he asked, carefully charring the tip of a cigar. 'How would you recover the loot?'

'The newspaper mentioned a family vault. Might not be too difficult.'

'*Hmm.* A plethora of supposition.' He drew on the cigar. 'But enough evidence to warrant action. I've set a forensic team to work on those skeletons. Your job is to get back to America.' He smiled blandly as I opened my mouth to protest. 'Save your breath, dear boy. I know what you're going to say. We have an agreement—right? So we do. So we do. But let me remind you—this situation is not of my making. It's *yours*—from first to last. Listen to this: *Doctor Meynell's action would seem to seriously compromise departmental activity in this theatre.* There you hear the authentic tones of Major Compton-Barryll— master of the split infinitive and member of our Military Attaché's staff in Washington. This is his report, commenting on your arrest in Reverence. In particular he takes exception to invoking the aid of Senator Patterson—a statesman grown garrulous with the passing years.'

'I had no reason to believe he'd be indiscreet.'

'Of course not, dear boy—but you do see the position. You've *upset* people. Poor Compton-Barryll is much displeased. Go and make your peace with him. I'm arranging for you to be formally accredited to the Washington office for liaison duties. You'll represent our interests in the Brandon investigation. A valuable exercise in international co-operation. The Americans may want to put a security blanket over the whole affair but you'll have to point out that it involves homicide cases on both sides of the Atlantic. See?—you do have your uses after all. MacTricycle will brief you, then you can away home to yet another night of bliss with your dear wife.'

'It's not that easy.'

He blinked. 'Don't look at me, dear boy—I'm no marriage guidance counsellor.' His humour was heavy-handed as ever.

'About going home,' I said patiently. '*Effendi?*'

He blew a stream of smoke towards the ceiling. 'The obnoxious Ottoman? Not a telescopic merchant is he?'

'Thirty-eight at close range.'

'Well—where's the problem? Shouldn't be too hard for you to keep out of trouble.'

'I'd feel more confident if Peters hadn't gone down. He knew how to take care of himself. Doesn't say much for my chances.'

He clasped well-manicured hands behind his head and settled more comfortably in his chair. 'Fret not thyself because of evil doers. See the duty armourer— he'll slip you a little something—and I've detailed Meek to cover you. Know him?'

'Should I?'

'Not specially. Very furtive is Meek—and utterly despicable of course. Be thankful he's on our side. Right? Well toddle along.' As I reached the door he added, 'You'll be taking Anne to America.'

'I will?'

'Question of economy, dear boy. Cheaper to put her on your expense account than give her protection here. She's your Achilles' heel.'

We reached the apartment without incident, paying off our cab two streets away and sneaking in through the communal garage and a flight of stone steps worn by the feet of Edwardian domestics. Someone had been busy sponging Peters' blood from the carpet outside our door.

The setting sun shone directly into our lounge-diner, slanting the length of once-genteel Tichborne Terrace where parked cars choked the gutter. For a sniper the room was a well-lit stage. I drew the heavy velvet curtains. In the gloom I could hear Anne moving behind me.

'I'm going to shower,' she said.

I blundered into a chair. 'Switch on the lights.'

She opened the door leading to the passage beyond which lay bedrooms and bathroom.

'David.'

Her voice was quiet—the hesitant almost apologetic tone she uses to announce a spider in the bath or a wasp in the kitchen.

I stumbled to her side.

The body of a man was taking up six feet of floor-space—flat on his back, eyes closed, a nimbus of greasy black hair standing out from his head. A smart grey jacket gaped open to reveal an empty leather holster under his left armpit. The lining of his pockets had been pulled out. Money, papers and a leather wallet lay beside him.

'Who is he?' Anne's voice betrayed no emotion.

I slid my Beretta from its resting-place in the waist-band of my cords, eased the safetycatch forward to expose the red warning mark and thumbed back the cocking lever. Its reassuring double *click* sounded very loud in that tiny passage.

'*No need for the popgun, squire.*' A man's voice from beyond our open bedroom door.

I pulled Anne back into the darkened lounge. 'Who's that?'

'Meek. I'm coming out—okay?'

'Make it slow and keep your hands where I can see them.'

A chuckle. 'Suit yourself, squire.' He emerged from the bedroom and stood at the far end of the passage—arms outstretched like the stone Christ above Rio. For someone the Director considered despicable he presented an unexpectedly conventional appearance—neat brown suit, quiet tie and immaculately polished brown leather shoes. His youthful black face wore a mocking grin. 'Satisfied?'

'How do I know that's not Meek down there?'

'I've a card in my pocket, dear Liza.'

'Show. *Very* slowly.'

He nodded. 'Cautious. I like that. Perhaps a bit *too* safety conscious, eh? Should have left the old musket cocked, squire. Safety catch is enough. It's quiet. Doesn't give the game away. And now—a roll of drums *if* you please. Unbutton jacket—*so*. Hold jacket open . . . remove ID wallet between thumb and forefinger—*so*. Notice that at no time does my hand leave my arm. Now—gently toss wallet in direction of professor, taking care not to arouse suspicion by any hasty or unexpected movement.'

It landed a foot from the door.

'Get it,' I whispered to Anne, 'and don't block my view.'

She knelt, picked it up and checked photograph and description. 'Relax. It's Meek.'

I stepped into the passage. 'Then who's *that*?'

He glanced at the body. 'Alfonso? Haven't a clue. Oh, don't worry. *Not dead, only sleeping*—as it say on ma old granpappy's grave. Found him nosing around when I came to give your place the once-over. Could this be the lad you're after?'

'Too young to be Effendi—but not too young to be his hit-man. Unless you've boobed and this boy's from the police.'

'Poncing around in that gear?' One gleaming shoe disdainfully lifted a lapel of the fallen man's jacket and then moved to scatter the money which lay beside him. 'And with a fistful of dollars? I think not.'

'You couldn't have known that when you clobbered him.'

His grin broadened. 'I'm psychic. If it'll make you feel any better, let's get him to a chair. About time he did some talking.'

I switched on some lights and between us we dragged the inert figure to our leather Chesterfield.

'Is he bleeding?' asked Anne.

Meek was affronted. 'Do me a favour! I'm not one of your brute-force-and-ignorance merchants. Just an anaesthetist, that's me—when I have to be.' The unconscious man grunted and moved his head. 'See? Sleepy-times are over. Best if you keep out of sight, squire. Let me ask the questions.'

The interrogation would have won no plaudits from Amnesty International. Meek set the scene swiftly, rigging my Anglepoise desklamp on a coffee table to shine directly into the man's face and turning off every other light in the room. Then he settled behind the lamp and waited. Another minute and the stranger was struggling to sit up.

'Don't move.' Meek's voice was gently solicitous.

'You just lie back nice and easy. Simple answers to simple questions—that's all we want. You don't even have to think. Just talk. *Name?*'

'Mickey Mouse.' American. I wasn't surprised.

Meek was unruffled. 'Hey—a comedian! The show needs a few laughs. Great little act you've got here, boy—like being in possession of explosive material, namely ammonium-nitrate fuel oil; being in possession of an offensive weapon, to wit one thirty-eight calibre revolver; having no current British licence for same; breaking and entering; being found on enclosed premises with intent to commit a felony; going equipped to commit burglary; threatening behaviour . . . Wow! When the jury hears that lot read out, the old clapometer will blow a fuse. They'll zap you, boy—they'll zap you real good. You'll go down for ten . . . maybe even rate twelve. We just love comics like you. Not laughing, Mickey? Maybe you're right. Twelve years in a British jail—no, that ain't funny.'

The man turned his head to avoid the glare. 'I was just looking the place over,' he muttered.

'Sure you were, Mickey—sure you were. With a thirty-eight . . . *anfo*—'

'Screw that!'

But we've got it, Mickey. No expense spared. So people are going to ask what outfit you work for. IRA? PLO? No—your face doesn't fit. How about the Red Brigades?'

'What is this? I never handled explosives in my life. It's a plant!'

'Like they say—tell that to the judge. We live in troubled times, Mickey. Pays to keep your nose clean.

You see how it is? Play games with us—we play games with you. What say we start over again, huh? *Name?*'

'Art Morino.'

'There—that wasn't hard, was it? Where d'you live, Arturo?'

'Bowdoin Landing—that's five miles out of Brunswick, Maine.'

'You're long ways from home, Arturo. Tell us about it.'

'I'm looking for a guy called Meynell.'

'Who's he?'

Morino shaded his eyes and tried to peer round the room. 'What kind of question is that? This is his pad.'

'And you want him?'

'My boss *wants*. I *fetch*.'

'Little doggie, huh? Now you pay attention, boy—this is the Royal Borough of Kensington. You seen the notices on the lamp-posts—all about how the owner gets clobbered if his dog fouls the sidewalk? You are a filthy little animal, Arturo. Who's got his name on your collar?'

Morino was recovering some shreds of dignity. He sat up, dusted his jacket and stuffed the lining back into his pockets.

But he said nothing.

I saw Meek quietly slide the coffee table aside with his left foot while one hand kept the lamp trained on the man's face.

'Don't keep me waiting, boy. Not polite. Who owns you?'

The room was very quiet. In another apartment a radio was belting out a hymn—*'This is my story, this is my song, Praising my Saviour all the day long . . .'*

Meek laughed softly—an ugly sound from the shadows. 'Play it your way, son—but you're going to tell me.'

'Get lost.'

A sudden flash of movement. Meek's right leg lashed out—the toe of his gleaming shoe catching Morino under the left kneecap.

'Mind you—' His voice cut through the injured man's noisy agony with the high clipped tone of a Sandhurst subaltern. '—one has to admire a fellow's loyalty.'

In the cab I said, 'We're all to blame. We go around turning up old stones—and expect someone like Meek to tread on whatever comes crawling out.'

Anne stared through the left-hand window at the Albert Memorial, its pinnacles sharp against a twilit sky. '*Tread* is right.'

'What was the alternative? Someone's out to kill me. Every scrap of information could be vital—and Morino sits there laughing at us.'

'He's not laughing now.'

'At this very moment Meek could be the charming host, plying young Arturo with our whisky. You saw how he was. Once he'd got what we wanted to hear, he was quite chummy with our little friend.'

I felt her shiver. 'That was as bad. David—that *frightened* me.'

'Professionalism. Ron Metcalfe could be just as ruthless—and you know what an easy-going chap he was, most of the time.'

The driver slid back his glass partition. 'You did say the Halton?'

I leaned forward. 'That's right. Piccadilly.'

'I know where it is, chief. Had a sudden thought you might have said *Hilton*. Bit of a difference.'

True. Once through its glazed revolving door we were among the potted palms and electroliers of a bygone age. Scant concession there to time's passing. Where other establishments welcomed guests in a blaze of fluorescence, the Halton preferred dim religious light. An anachronism, the place had survived to enjoy new popularity in the raging nostalgia epidemic of the late seventies.

Third floor. *The Osborne Suite*. I eased the door and let it swing open to reveal an Edwardian period-piece beyond. Dark mahogany against a backdrop of heavy maroon drapes. In a large wing-chair sat the man we had come to see—bearded, grey-haired and engrossed in a girlie magazine. An old-gold quilted smoking-jacket relieved sombre black and white evening dress and brought a hint of decadence—eloquent of something Oscar Wilde might have wished he'd said. On the far wall a mirror confirmed that he was alone.

'Mr Spreight,' I said. 'You have something to tell me?'

CHAPTER
ELEVEN

His piggy eyes lifted from a photograph in which a young woman appeared to be scratching an embarrassing itch. 'You have the advantage of me, sir.' He glanced towards Anne and recognition dawned. 'Ah—Doctor Meynell, I presume? I was not expecting you tonight. This is hardly the hour for social calls.'

His air of polite reproof infuriated me. 'I don't need lessons in etiquette from you, Spreight. You want to see me? I'm here. You've something to say? Say it— but make it fast. Five minutes from now I'm calling the police. You sent an armed man to burgle my apartment. That your idea of a social call?'

'I—' a hairline crack opened in his brittle façade of composure. 'What are you talking about?'

'Art Morino—and don't tell me you've never heard of him.'

'Why should I do that? I employ him.'

'As muscle.'

He blinked. 'As my *aide*, Doctor.'

'Two hours ago he broke into our apartment—on your instructions.'

'That I most strenuously deny.' He waved towards a couple of easy chairs. 'Look, can't we discuss this in a civilized manner. You're clearly under a grave misapprehension. I have high regard for you, sir—as indeed I have for Mrs Meynell. Her father is one of my most valued advisers. Sit down, both of you. There . . . that's better. Now exactly what has Morino done?'

'He says you sent him to fetch me. That's his excuse for being in our apartment.'

Spreight shook his head sadly. 'I fear my efforts on that young man's behalf are wasted. From the gutter he came. To the gutter he will assuredly return. I sent him to *find* you, Doctor. The word *fetch* was never included in my instructions. You see, sir, I have been most concerned about you. The more so since the regrettable death of Peters.'

'You know about that?'

'Indeed I do—as is only fitting since I also employed him.' He saw my surprise. 'You were not aware of that? But I was under the impression he made that clear when he spoke to you the other day at Hampton University. Obviously he omitted to do so. Oh yes, I retained his services when I visited Reverence last week. District Attorney Cook mentioned him as the man responsible for recovering the missing *objets d'art*. That was enough recommendation for me. I was leaving for England next day—I'm over here for the Henry Moore exhibitions and in the hope of commissioning a work—and I wanted someone to represent my interests in Reverence. I need hardly say upon *what* those interests are centred.'

'The Pompadour Vase,' said Anne.

'Precisely. Then *you* appeared on the scene, Doctor. Truly a gift from the gods. A man of culture . . . an archaeologist skilled in the art of investigation—and married to a charming woman whose expertise in the field of antiques must amply fill any *lacunae* in your knowledge. When Peters told me you had declined what—in all charity—I must call the insulting attempt of Vincent Goring to recruit your services, I admit I began to cherish hopes that you and I might co-operate in this venture of mine. I have no interest in the unhappy and sordid events in Reverence—except to rejoice that they have brought the other Pompadour back into the light of day. My one concern is to obtain that vase legitimately and—since I am no longer a young man—speedily.'

My mind was blinking at the new light flooding the situation. 'What you call your *venture* can't be divorced from the murder investigation in Reverence.'

'Indeed it cannot—as poor Peters found to his cost. Ironic . . . he left Goring's employment because of that specific conflict of interests.'

'I heard he was fired.'

'Then you were misinformed, Doctor. Peters discovered that the foolish young man Kendrick had an accomplice—a wretched creature whose name escapes me.'

'Ollie Piper.'

'The name is unimportant. What *is* important is that this petty criminal had possessed himself of vital evidence about the vase. Peters called Goring to see if a financial arrangement could be made whereby that evidence could be secured. You know about this?'

I nodded. 'And before the deal could be set up, Ollie Piper was killed.'

'Under highly suspicious circumstances. Consider, Doctor—the man was in hiding. Peters found him. The fact that he found him *alive* suggests that nobody else knew of his hiding-place. Peters called Goring and because a licensed investigator may not be party to any deal which might pervert the course of justice, he told Goring where this man could be located and left him to make his own arrangements. Within half an hour, the man was dead. Now—do you wonder that Peters was anxious to sever all connexion with Goring and his associates?'

I saw again that dark green Cadillac racing down the drive from Kendrick's house, tyres squealing as it hit the road to Reverence. Whoever sat behind its tinted windows must have been bent on Ollie Piper's destruction.

'So when Peters came to see me at Hampton he already suspected one of the Fairfield bunch?'

Spreight's thin lips parted to reveal too-perfect teeth. '*The Fairfield bunch*,' he echoed. 'You have a ready turn of phrase, Doctor—but the terminology of the old West is hardly apt to describe directors of a multi-million-dollar corporation. There are similarities, but these men are not likely to shield one of their number suspected of murder. How shall I put it?— their loyalty to Fairfield will always override any loyalty to the—ah—*bunch*.'

'If Peters had levelled with me, he might be alive now. I assumed he was still working for Goring. When Mrs Kendrick called, last Thursday, I told her he'd been to see me—mentioned the evidence he'd got from Ollie Piper . . . Hugh Annandale's letter. She'd pass all that to Goring.'

He placed his fingertips together. '*Hugh Annandale?* You've been busy. Can it be you've already espoused my cause?'

'No it can't,' exclaimed Anne hotly. 'My husband isn't doing this so you can add to your collection. He's doing it to stay alive!'

'She's right,' I said. 'Before Peters died he warned me I'm in line for a bullet from the man to whom Annandale wrote that letter. Incidentally—when were *you* at Danton Court?'

'Forty years ago—almost to the day. You *have* learned a lot—and in such a short time. I knew I was doing the right thing when I asked Peters to sound you out. And don't look so grim, Doctor—I assure you there was nothing sinister about my visit to Danton. I went there to examine . . . oh, something or other. Chairs, I think. Annandale was already stripping the place. I didn't buy anything but I did see the Pompadour Vase. He was very proud of it—and rightly so. When I identified it as Tournier he was delighted—insisted on telling me its entire history, including that incredibly boring episode during the Peninsular War. But the thing was a family heirloom. No sale—though I tried my damnedest. I fear I wore out my welcome. One thing he omitted to tell me was that there are *two* vases. When *my* Pompadour came onto the market I was convinced it was his. I read the Knoll-Bertrand catalogue—and the history there was almost identical to what I'd heard, except that the name of the English owner was Cobley. That had me puzzled until I saw that Theo Shelling bought the vase in England in thirty-eight—the very year old Annandale was telling me he'd never sell. I reasoned that the name Cobley was a ruse to cover the seller's identity. It happens. Then I met Theo at the sale and he left me in no doubt that the facts he'd been given were correct. But my heart was set on that vase—as you may judge from the price I paid. Fierce bidding, Doctor—*fierce* . . . and I'll swear nobody else in that room even guessed the existence of the second Pompadour.' He smiled at the memory.

Convinced, I asked what Peters was doing in England.

'Looking for you, Doctor. After he spoke with you at Hampton he called me here in London—told me of the new evidence he'd discovered . . . that he'd parted company with Goring . . . and that you had agreed to undertake an investigation over here. As I understood it, you knew you would be collaborating in my own venture. Courtesy demanded we all meet—you, Peters and I. I'm a cautious man, Doctor. I've learned the folly of putting pen to paper in circumstances where discretion is paramount. So since Peters had already—as I imagined—acted as my emissary to you, I left him to make the arrangements for our meeting. I told him to get over here—my Boston lawyers would provide the money—contact you and ask you to call me. He arrived on the noon flight yesterday . . . checked in at the Burgoyne Towers where I'd booked a room for him. That's where he was shot.'

'The police know all this?'

'Naturally. They were here last night—having traced me through that booking at the Burgoyne Towers. Ridiculous though this may sound, I believe they actually thought *I* was responsible for Peters' death.'

I remembered that dying whisper. *'He'll try for you next. Has to. Spreight's paying . . .'* Peters was telling me Spreight had paid for him to come to London and find me.

'Was Peters bringing you the evidence he'd found on Ollie Piper?' I asked.

'But of course. It's of the greatest importance.'

'It wasn't on him when his body was searched at the morgue. Had his room been turned over?'

'By the man who killed him? I imagine so. The police asked if he were carrying anything valuable.'

'And you told them—?'

Spreight bridled. 'Admit that a man in my employment was bringing evidence which should rightly be in the hands of the Reverence Police Department? My sense of public duty has limits, Doctor.'

'So it's possible Effendi thinks he's in the clear. He knew what was inside his Pompadour Vase—so he followed Peters, hoping to recover those two scraps of paper which could betray him. He wasn't interested in Peters—only the evidence. Big question: Where was it? No point getting rid of Peters if the evidence was going to turn up again. Then he found out that Peters was coming to England. How? Probably called his office. *'Sorry, Mr Peters is off to London'.* That could mean Peters was bringing the evidence over here for me to see.'

Spreight raised a hand to interrupt. 'I appreciate that your suppositions are bound to be subjective, Doctor, but since *I* was retaining Peters' services, it would be more reasonable to assume he was bringing the evidence to *me*.' He leaned back, hands clasped across his stomach.

'But nobody knew he was working for you. On the other hand, I'd already told Mrs Kendrick I was ready to help Peters with the investigation.'

'*Hmph!*' He tossed his head—a spoiled child.

'So Effendi goes after Peters. Books a London flight—'

'On the same plane,' suggested Anne. 'Otherwise how would he find Peters in London?' She saw my expression. 'What's wrong, David?'

I sighed. '*That's* wrong. Peters being followed every step of the way. The man was a pro. He'd *know*. All the way from New York to London. . . ?'

'*Boston*,' Spreight corrected. 'Peters flew from Boston.'

My shoulders sagged. 'There you are. How could Effendi know? The airport . . . the plane—no, it's too smooth.'

'But it *happened*,' said Anne doggedly. 'Peters is dead—and Effendi's here.'

'I wonder. He's got what he came for—the evidence Peters was carrying. Why hang around here? He's supposed to be in Reverence, so he can't risk staying away too long. I reckon he's headed back to the States.'

'But we have copies of that evidence.'

'He doesn't know that.'

Her eyes were bright. 'Tell you something else—I'll bet he doesn't know Peters lived long enough to talk to us.'

Spreight stroked his quilted jacket. 'How can you be sure of that, Mrs Meynell?'

'Because . . . because—' Her excitement was mounting. '—he must have thought he'd killed him there in that hotel room. Would he have left him like that if he'd thought he was still alive?'

'Why not? Your husband has already pointed out that the man wasn't interested in Peters—only in securing that evidence.'

'But don't you see? *Peters saw who shot him.* He could identify Effendi. That's what he was trying to tell us when he died.'

'Only he didn't make it,' I said gloomily. 'When I think of him struggling across London in that condition. . . .' I shook my head. 'If he'd called a doctor he might be alive now.'

Anne bit her lip. 'Maybe things aren't as hopeless as you think,' she said.

I looked at her sharply but her eyes said *Later*.

We called our apartment and told Meek to put the damaged Morino out on the street. Hearing Spreight's grim prognosis of his henchman's immediate future I pitied the wretched Art. He had simply conformed to type—forcing an entry and prowling through our deserted rooms in search of some clue to our whereabouts. Now—the price of a fare home. And home would never again be Spreight's mansion at Bowdoin Landing.

We left the Osborne Suite and sank to street level in a genteel mirror-panelled lift. Out in Piccadilly the warm night was alive with traffic noise.

Anne said, 'Let's walk. With Meek as house-guest there's no chance for private conversation at home.'

I took her hand. 'Converse away.' We strolled slowly towards Hyde Park.

'It's not easy.' A long silence. 'David—d'you like living in London?'

I was unprepared for that. 'Haven't thought about it much. Why?'

She took a deep breath. 'I'd like to move.'

'You don't like the apartment?'

'I *did*—but it's getting so I'm afraid to go back there. We've been burglarized. We found Dan Peters literally dying on our doorstep. And tonight was the *end*. I mean it, David. That room will never be the same. I'll always see that awful little man writhing about on the carpet.'

'That *little* man was a six-footer.'

'I'm *serious*.'

'All right—so we find another apartment . . . another town . . . another continent.'

She misunderstood. 'Don't be cross—*please*.'

I stood still and caught her shoulders. She was my wife—tired . . . upset . . . still wearing clothes put on thirty-six hours before. They were crumpled because she had slept cramped in the back of Angus's tiny three-wheeler—and I had dragged her out to confront Spreight without time to change. She had not complained. Suddenly I didn't give a damn about Spreight . . . Effendi . . . the Pompadour Vase . . . or the Director and all his works.

I held her close—there in the middle of Piccadilly,

London, England—where men approaching middle life who need glasses and find they tire more easily now are not expected to do such things. Certainly not with their wives. 'I'm not cross.' My voice was playing tricks. 'Just *sorry*. I've been a thoughtless oaf—prancing up and down the length of England, expecting you to don cap and bells and keep me company. What sort of crazy life is this, anyway? We're expected to invite people into our home and then sit around watching them kick other people's kneecaps. I buy a television licence for that kind of entertainment. We don't want it spilling out all over the lounge. Right! I'm crying *Hold! Enough!* You want to move house? Okay—where's it to be?'

There were tears in her eyes. 'I *love* you,' she said. Then, wistfully, 'But tomorrow you'll be back at work.'

I expressed myself forcefully on that subject.

'David! You can't just—well, do *that* to your work. Maybe when this job's over. . . .'

'*When!*' I felt deflated. 'Now—this moment—we know Effendi is one of Goring's crowd.'

'We do?'

'You heard what Spreight said. Peters suspected it when Ollie Piper was killed—and he died warning me I'm the next target. But who knows I'm involved? The Fairfield Bunch. It has to be one of them. Give me time and I'll come up with the right name. So what does the Department do? It ships me off to Washington to do penance while Effendi is busy covering his tracks.'

She stepped back and looked into my eyes. 'You

really want to finish this job your own way? It's that important?'

Peters blood was still on my sleeve. I could see it in the lamplight. 'It's personal.'

'Then stop waiting for things to happen. Get Effendi out in the open.' She was still watching me closely. *'Tell him the one thing he doesn't want to hear.'*

CHAPTER
TWELVE

Meek had prepared food. It seemed an age since Timothy Brice's mess of pottage—and time is a great healer. The two meals were as sharply contrasted as their creators. We sat by candlelight to savour *haute cuisine* while Meek expounded the virtues of his own special white wine sauce—as if anxious to exorcise the darker memories of that evening. The effort was wasted on Anne. She sat across from me, her face pale . . . shadows beneath her eyes. This facet of Meek's character disturbed her, as had his earlier *bonhomie* towards the bruised Morino. You never knew where you were with Meek. That's what kept him alive.

Just after eleven the phone rang. *'Your personal call to Vincent Goring in Reverence. Hold the line please.'* A pause. *'Go ahead, caller.'*

'Mr Goring? David Meynell.'

'Doctor! Surprise, surprise. What's new?'

'Peters is dead. Shot yesterday—here in London.'

Close beside me Anne pressed her ear against the phone to catch that distant voice. 'My God! I thought he was still in Reverence. What was he doing over there?'

'On his way to my place with fresh evidence about the Kendrick killing.'

'I don't get it, Doctor. He wasn't working for us. Are you saying he was still on the case?'

'Seems so. The important thing is—he wasn't killed outright. He talked.'

Another silence as Goring pondered the implications of what I had said.

'Go on, Doctor.' He spoke very slowly. 'What did he tell you?'

'Enough for us to identify who shot him—and killed Matt Kendrick.'

'Let's get this straight, Doctor. You actually *know*?' There was a new note in his voice. Long-distance it sounded like mockery.

'I didn't say that, Mr Goring. Peters gave us a lead. We're following it up, but with your help we'll move faster.'

'*My* help? How come?'

'We need a name—and it'll save us a lot of sweat if you can give us something to go on. The man we want is someone Peters knew by sight. Lives on Olivet. Possible Fairfield connections. And in the army just after World War Two.'

'Hold it—I'm getting that down. *Olivet . . . Fairfield . . . army after the war*. Anything else?'

'That's about it.'

'Hell, with those qualifications it could be one of us five.'

My laugh was meant to sound genuine. 'I wouldn't be calling if I believed that. But I'm sure you'll come up with the name we want. How soon, d'you reckon?'

'Well now, it's not that easy, Doctor. Any other time I'd just pick up this phone, call my associates, and we'd be in business. But right now things are difficult. Walter's over in Paris, France. Grant's grabbing a few days vacation down in Florida. Don't know about Foster and Paul. I only got in from New York an hour ago. Been there since Friday, so I'm a bit out of touch. See what I can do. I sure as hell am sorry about Peters. We had a slight difference of opinion, but he was a first-rate investigator. I forget—do we have your number?'

I gave it to him. 'And I'll call you again if there's anything new. We have a couple more leads but they'll have to be followed up over here. Could be we'll beat you to it, even now.'

'That close, huh?' He could have sounded more enthusiastic.

'Just one other point, Mr Goring. A dark green Cadillac with tinted windows. At the Kendrick house, the day of Matt's funeral. Who owns it?'

'That'll be one of the Corporation cars. Guess someone had it brought round in case it was needed after the funeral.'

'It was.' I left it at that.

I put the phone down to a slow handclap from Meek. 'Oh *jolly* good show, squire. Flushing him out, are we?'

I noted the time of the call on a pad of official forms. Whitehall auditors thrive on such detail. 'I'm not hopeful. The Fairfield Bunch are scattered. Walter Cornhill's in Paris. Grant Aitken's on holiday in Florida. Goring's only just back from New York.'

Anne said, 'You believe that?'

'Shouldn't I?'

'Could be he's just back from London, England. Or—even if he's telling the truth—how can he be sure about the others? And what about Paul Chaimer and Myra's father? If Goring really has been away since the funeral, he doesn't know where they are or what they've been doing.'

'Know what *I* admired?' Meek was grinning. 'I really did admire your attention to detail. You want an ex-army man who was still serving *just after* the war. That *really* sounds authentic.'

'So it should. We have to convince our man we're on the right track—that we know he was involved in exhuming General Brandon's body.'

He stared at me blankly. 'Sorry squire—I'm not with you. Fill me in. Anything to do with the opposition interests me.'

While Anne made fresh coffee I told him what we had learned at Imberbridge. He sat hunched forward, slowly brushing one palm across the other, staring at the pale skin as if reading the future in its creases.

'That description . . .' He was frowning. 'The plane crash. Vivid. Eye-witness?'

'Hugh Annandale?'

'That figures. But all the other detail—the flight in the Sunderland . . . the diversion to Belfast—did Annandale come up with that lot too?'

'Don't see how he could. The reporter would get that from . . .' I was guessing—'transcripts of the official enquiry?'

He was picking at a hardened blister on his left hand. 'That the way you figure it?'

'It's a reasonable assumption.'

'Oh sure—*now*. The bookshops are full of them—war stories, documented right down to when the tail gunner went for a slash. But—nineteen forty-seven? Defence of the Realm Act and all that cock? Come on, squire—you're supposed to be the expert. Would a reporter on some local rag have access to that kind of information?'

He was talking sense. 'Okay,' I said. 'So Annandale . . . No—that doesn't fit either. He wouldn't know. *Nobody* would know—I mean really *know*. If nobody survived the crash, all those details about that last flight are pure imagination—dreamed up on a hack reporter's typewriter.'

From the kitchen Anne said, 'How do you know there weren't any survivors? David—this could be the link we're needing! When was that crash?'

'Forty-three. July.'

She brought the coffee in. 'And when did Hugh Annandale write that letter? You told me that was in forty-three. The day Italy surrendered, you said—or just after. Don't you see? The pilot—suppose he crawled out of the airplane. Annandale was there. He'd help him. And if the man survived, isn't it likely he'd come back later to say Thank you? And isn't it likely old Annandale might show him the Pompadour Vase?'

Meek slid his cup towards the coffee-pot. 'That's one "*isn't it likely*" on another "*isn't it likely*" on a "*suppose*". Wishful thinking, Mrs Meynell.'

In bed I lay awake while Anne slept. The digital display on our alarm radio flickered green—the figures blurred to my strained eyes. Two o'clock—the hour for doubt and depression.

How could Peters be sure the man who shot him was Effendi? Was the reason for that nickname so obvious? I had checked the dictionary:

> effendi, *e-fen'di*, n. a title for civil officials and educated persons generally (abolished in Turkey in 1934). (Turk.; from Gr. *authentēs*, an absolute master.)

Annandale had called Oberon Spreight *The Fairy King*—using the name of his subject rather than any physical characteristic as basis for verbal humour.

Lying there in the darkness I checked our list of suspects for a name suggesting authority. *Cornhill* . . . *Chaimer* . . . *Durrell* . . . *Aitken*—nothing there. *Goring?* That was a name to conjure with during World War Two. Reichmarschall Herman Goering—undoubtedly the Luftwaffe's *Supremo*. But the allusion was obscure—seldom the case with nicknames—and would Hugh Annandale jest on what could have been a sensitive matter at that time?

How about first names? Here Aitken qualified with *Grant*—recalling the Civil War general.

If the nickname originated with Annandale—and we had no proof of that—could we hope to understand its significance without some insight into his mind? He had served in Egypt and the Sudan when *Effendi* was still widely used as a term of respect. What memories might prompt its bestowal on a young American rescued from that crashed Piper?

If there ever were such a survivor.

If he were Effendi.

If he had anything to do with the theft of the Pompadour Vase, four years later.

If. . .

I fell asleep pondering unresolved questions.

Someone was shaking my arm gently but persistently. *'We got ourselves a visitor.'* Meek's voice—little more than a breath in my ear.

I eased out of bed without disturbing Anne, grabbed some clothes and followed him into the darkened lounge. He pointed to a gap between the curtains through which amber glare from the street-lamps struck up at the ceiling. 'Arrived about quarter of an hour ago. Dodged into a doorway on the corner over there . . . watched this place for five minutes— then came across. I nipped along to the stairs—heard him moving around on the ground floor. Sounded like he was trying a door at the back. Then he went out again.'

'You followed him?'

'Do me a favour, squire. If this charley's a pro, that's just what he'd want. He'd have an oppo waiting to nip in, soon as I'd gone. Come on—let's take a shufti round the back.'

Outside the apartment I whispered, 'You reckon he's a pro?'

'Noise he was making downstairs I'd have said a rank amateur—but that may have been to get me out in the open.'

The passage was in darkness. We crept soundlessly to the door opening onto stone stairs at the back of the building. Carefully Meek eased it on its hinges—just wide enough to peer out. Pale light through that narrow crack showed the silenced revolver in his right hand. 'Clear,' he breathed—and opened the door wider.

A cool breeze brushed my face. The stairs had been built against the apartment block with a brick wall for balustrade. Across the way, light gleamed from a first-floor window while the false dawn of that July morning struggled to dim the hazy glow of London's streetlamps. But in the well between the tall buildings all was darkness.

A slight sound—like the friendly *chink* of bottle on glass—scuttered up the stairway.

Meek touched my arm. 'He's on his way.'

I leaned closer to him. 'Watch it. Could be the police keeping an eye on the place.'

He drew a sharp breath like the hiss of a snake. 'Got your shooter?'

'I—' My hands were empty.

His mouth was against my ear. 'Then don't try teaching me my job.'

Stealthy footsteps crept nearer. We stared down to where the flight turned back on itself and disappeared. Suddenly, in the shadows, a figure eased cautiously from the wall.

Meek's gun came up. '*Security! Hold it right there!*'

But even as he spoke the figure vanished. Frantic steps pattering away beneath us . . . a moment's silence . . . the sound of breaking glass—then steps again, hurrying across the courtyard towards the garage and the street beyond. Seconds later a car door slammed and the roar of an engine faded on the morning air.

'Frightened him off,' I said.

Meek shrugged. 'Don't bet on it. Could be like I said—one at the back, one at the front.'

In the bedroom I found the light on and Anne in her dressing-gown. She looked at me anxiously. 'I heard somebody shouting.'

'Meek.' I pulled the Beretta from under my pillow. 'We've had a caller.'

A tap at the door. 'Spare a minute, squire?'

'I'm coming too,' said Anne emphatically.

Meek led us back to the stone stairs. 'Sniff.'

'Gasoline.' 'Petrol.' Anne and I spoke together.

He nodded. 'Same difference. Come on—let's see the damage.'

Two flights down—a broken bottle with a length of petrol-soaked rag still sticking from its neck. The would-be arsonist lay beside his shattered missile. Meek shone a torch and turned the body over on its back.

'Well, well,' he said. 'Our little bundle of laughs.'

Morino—a bullet through his heart.

CHAPTER
THIRTEEN

The police came . . . questioned . . . photographed—
then bore Morino's body like Hamlet from the stage.
Meek they did not like, nor he them. An armed agent
in close proximity to a bullet-punctured corpse? *'ullo,
'ullo, 'ullo!* And I collected odd glances. Peters at the
front door . . . Morino at the back—men marked for
death were stumbling to my apartment as elephants to
their legendary graveyard.

At five, when the champions of law and order departed, we sat drinking coffee and reconstructing the
events which had troubled our short night. The police
theory: Morino brought an accomplice who panicked,
fired the fatal shot and took off. The alternative—an
incendiary and a killer, strangers to each other, both
picking the same place . . . the same night . . . the
same time—that was coincidence beyond constabu-
lary belief.

We thought otherwise. July. Short nights; little time
when Kensington streets were deserted, its citizens
abed. For men needing those conditions, three in the
morning provided the optimum.

Morino's purpose—straight revenge. Intent on
lobbing a Molotov cocktail through our window, he
would approach through the garage and across the
courtyard, unaware that only yards behind, another
man pursued an equally lawless mission. Morino was

near the top of the stairs as that other man began his ascent. Meek's warning—loud . . . clear . . . echoing down into the dark well between the buildings— startled both men. The prowler on the lower flight, hearing urgent footsteps . . . suddenly confronted by the fleeing Morino, would assume this was an armed security guard. One shot from a silenced gun . . . the shattering of glass as the petrol-bomb smashed . . . then the footsteps of the killer escaping.

Effendi. By the pricking of my thumbs I *knew*.

Anne said, 'So he wasn't satisfied with recovering that evidence from Peters. He won't stop till he's got to you.'

Meek ladled sugar into his coffee. 'Killing the prof here won't solve anything—not now the Department's involved.'

'He doesn't know that,' I reminded him.

'So he doesn't know about the Department—but he must realise you've talked to *somebody*. He's not dim, squire. In his place I'd do a quick fade. When your cover's blown you don't waste time picking off the opposition—you get out fast.'

'Sure—*when* your cover's blown. But we still don't know who he is. We know who he *isn't*, though— which is something. Cross Goring off. No way could he take my call in Reverence at eleven and be in London now.'

'Paul Chaimer too,' said Anne. 'You told me he's around forty. Too young to have been through World War Two in uniform.'

The phone rang. Duty Officer at the Ministry. 'Thought you'd better know, sir—we're having temporary stand-down on your American trip. The Yanks won't wear it. Very grateful for the info about General Brandon and all that, but seems they prefer to handle things on their own. Bit snooty about it, I'm afraid. Thought I'd better let you know straight away. Save you packing and all that.'

'I haven't *un*packed yet.'

'Oh? Ah. Yes. Oh—and one other thing. The Old Man says not to bother coming in till we call. Stay by the phone. State of readiness and all that. The Yanks could change their minds. We're working on it.'

'Don't strain yourselves. And switch me through to a recorder. I want to report an incident and you'd better have my version before the police come up with their's. . . .'

We spent the morning tidying the apartment while Meek snatched a few hours sleep under an eiderdown in the guest room. I found myself looking at the place with new eyes—the way Anne must see it . . . familiar . . . full of happy memories, yet soiled by recent events. I watched her busily dusting and rearranging the furniture—a slim figure in grey slacks and the old paint-spotted pink shirt she wears for housework; her golden hair hidden under a faded blue Breton cap.

'What you were saying last night . . .' I began. 'About moving house. Any suggestions?'

She stepped back from straightening a picture. 'At this moment in time—as far away as possible.'

'Like you might be saying . . . Stateside?'

She grinned. 'Like I might *not* be saying. It wouldn't work, David. You'd do it to please me, and I'd finish up with a guilt complex, watching you eat your heart out.'

'*Ugh*. And you know me better than that. I travel hopefully. Besides, we'd be together and—'

'—you'd *still* be unhappy. That I couldn't take. Darling, I know you better than you think. Sure, you travel well but you won't transplant easy. I guess I knew that when I married you but I only faced up to it two years ago when there was a chance of that Hampton appointment.'

'Chance? *Certainty!* Your father had it all sewn up.'

'And you made it sound like that's why you wouldn't take the job. But deep down I think you realized you wouldn't be happy living outside England. You need to know that just up the road there's an ancient British camp . . . a Roman city . . . a Norman castle—or just an old village pub.'

'Tudor—with Restoration barmaids.'

She smiled. 'I'm talking sense.'

'I think . . . I think you're indulging in your national pastime—analysis.'

'*You* . . !' Her clenched fists beat a playful tattoo on my chest. '*You Limey*—'

'*Ssh!*' I grabbed her in a bear-hug. 'Meek needs his beauty-sleep.'

She relaxed and leaned against me. 'I guess I'm not cut out to be the kind of wife who helps her man get ahead.' Her voice was muffled. 'I tried. I tried pushing you into that Hampton job—but I just couldn't do it.'

I lifted the Breton cap and tossed it away, resting my face against her soft hair. 'Because you knew it wouldn't work. But things can't just drift on like this. Right now the Old Man's rubbing his podgy hands because he thinks he's got me by the short and curlies. Two years . . . no heavy stuff—he's kept his word. *I'm* the one who's blown it—involved the Department in a purely personal matter. I go busting in on poor old Angus demanding action from the Department because I've suddenly become a target. I am a *fool*. Next week . . . next month . . . the Old Man's coming round for his pound of flesh.'

'He's already had that.' Her fingers moved across my shoulder-blade to the scar left by a Turkish surgeon's probing.

'So what's to do? Dean Ruskin's talking about a visiting professorship, but—'

'I didn't know that!'

'Haven't had time to think about it since we got back. He'd *like* a Chair of British Studies but the Governors won't wear that—so he's going for a Visiting Professor. Month in the fall; month in the spring; fieldwork over here in the summer.'

She stared. 'I don't *believe* it. You've known about this for days—yet you haven't said a word. David, how *could* you?'

'Didn't know how you'd take it—after I turned down the other Hampton appointment. Besides, nothing may come of it.'

'Nonsense. Dean Ruskin wouldn't say, if he wasn't confident of swinging it. Does Daddy know?'

'Has to—he's one of the Governors. But he's not going to push. And neither, my chick, are you. I only mention it now so you'll know I'm serious about packing things in at the Department. Right—where d'you want to live?'

So we spread maps on the floor and forgot the time until Meek stuck his woolly head round the door and asked plaintively about lunch.

While we ate, the sun blazed down—as it always does, first day back at work after a vacation. But I was not at work; I was waiting for Effendi to make another move. He was out there—I knew it—itching to get me in his sights. And growing desperate. Last night proved that. I had only to wait. He would come.

The two-tone chime had Meek on his feet, gun in hand. At the door I squinted through the discreet peephole lens.

On our threshold, a tall figure dwarfed as through the wrong end of a telescope—Walter Cornhill.

'I'm no fool, Doctor.' He was settled in an armchair with a cup of coffee on the low table at his side. 'You may have convinced Vincent that none of us is under suspicion but I know better. And if I had any doubts, my reception here makes the position perfectly clear.'

'We have to take precautions.'

'I recognise a peephole when I see one. You knew who I was—yet you had me covered and frisked before you put in an appearance. I'm not blaming you, but it proves my point—the man you want is one of *us*; one of the five you met at Myra's.'

'The man *you* want,' I reminded him.

'*Touché*. And for that reason I'm asking you to call off this investigation right now.'

Anne's cup clattered into its saucer. 'Four men

dead . . . David next in line—and you say call it off?'

He gave a thin smile. 'I phrased that badly. I wasn't meaning your husband should abandon the investigation—just don't turn it into a private party. Give us the chance to take an active part. Our purpose in asking for his help was to protect the good name of Fairfield Corporation. That still holds—whatever the cost. He obviously thinks one of us is responsible for killing Matt Kendrick . . . Piper . . . Peters—did you say *four* men? Who—?'

'You wouldn't know him,' I said. 'Nothing to do with the vase. He just got in the way—and that tells you a lot about the man we're up against.'

'Don't look at me! I've been in Paris, France since the day after Matt's funeral.'

'I'd heard. You in Paris . . . Goring in New York . . . Aitken in Florida—your police are very accommodating.'

'You mean "*Don't leave town*"? Life's not like they show it on television, Doctor. Brand's a realist—so is the DA. You can't impose that kind of restriction. Reverence needs Fairfield as a going concern. That means business must go on—wherever it takes us. It took me to Latourette Laboratories. Call them if you want to check. When I wasn't in conference I was home with their president. Flew into London this morning for a session with ICI tomorrow. Foster's joining me from the States later today. I spoke with Vincent in Reverence less than an hour ago and he told me about your call last evening. I know you suspect one of us—but I'm in the clear.'

'Convince me.'

His eyes glinted dangerously. 'You have my word. Let me remind you—as a lawyer—that it rests with you to establish guilt, rather than vice versa.'

'Circumstances alter cases.'

He closed his eyes for a moment and rubbed a finger pensively between his brows. 'All right—but at least let me know what I'm supposed to have done.'

'You were in the army.'

A nod. 'Legal branch. And if you're going to ask if I was still serving after the war, the answer's Yes. I was at the Nuremburg trials . . . stayed on in Europe for a while with the Judge Advocate's Department . . . got back to the States just before Christmas forty-six.'

'Discharged?'

He made a balancing gesture with his hands. 'Half and half. Officially on leave—but already getting back into civilian harness. I'd met up with Grant Aitken— knew him when he was with the Eighth over here— and he fixed for me to see Vincent Goring. That's how I came to handle Fairfield business. My army discharge didn't come through until May.'

'You were in the States all that time?'

'Unless you count a trip to Havana early in the new year. I guess you might call it a second honeymoon.' He gently tugged the lobe of his right ear. 'Doesn't seem all that time ago.'

I was puzzled. 'Yet you weren't discharged from the army till May.'

'You have to understand how it was, Doctor. We had a whole bunch of older men on the legal staff. They were back in civilian practice almost as soon as hostilities ended in forty-five. That meant a hell of a lot of work for those who were left. Even after that trip to Havana I found myself back in uniform for a couple of brief tours—mostly handling formalities for bringing home some of our war dead.'

'Like . . . General Brandon?'

His surprise was genuine—or he was a brilliant actor. 'How in the world did you know that? You're dead right—the General's exhumation was my very last assignment as a serving officer.'

'You said you didn't leave the States.'

'But that's right. I only handled the legal preliminaries. Your English law requires an order from the Home Secretary before a body can be exhumed. That's granted on application from the deceased's next of kin. General Brandon died a bachelor. No close family. But the people of his home town wanted their local hero brought back to the Brandon vault in Hatchfield. So the army took over the legal formalities.'

If he were telling the truth, the pieces were beginning to click together.

'When did you make those arrangements?'

He put a hand to his head. 'Let's see . . . it took some time. First the application to your Home Secretary, then fixing a date . . . I guess it took the whole of February—maybe into March.'

'And at that time you were already working with the Fairfield Corporation in Reverence.'

He smiled. 'Let's say I had a foot in the door. Officially I couldn't have a civilian job until after my discharge—but you know the way these things are done.'

I nodded. 'You talked about the Brandon exhumation?'

'In Reverence? Guess I must have. It wasn't classified information.'

So—what did we have? On January 10, 1947 Effendi opens his New York Times and reads that a Pompadour Vase, twin to the one he saw in Danton Court, has just fetched $11,000. Within weeks he learns that General Brandon's body is to be exhumed from Imberbridge churchyard. Was that when he began to plan a robbery which would lead to multiple murder?

I glanced at Cornhill sipping his coffee, his face a lawyer's expressionless mask. He had presented his case. *Consider your verdict.* Leaving him to Anne's small-talk and Meek's watchful eyes I used the extension phone in our bedroom to call Pennick at the Home Office. We had greeted each other across many a reopened grave in the past, he representing his lords and masters, I mine. About his bowler-hatted form clung the churchyard atmosphere of swirling early-morning mist and damp earth. Not surprisingly he was a martyr to colds, chills and influenza. My request for information was hailed with a shattering sneeze.

'Loog here, Beydell,' he protested hoarsely, 'this is a bid *thig*. Id's the biddle of the holiday seasod. There's odely a skeledod staff here.' Another sneeze. 'All ride—leave it with be. I'll call you bag.'

I knew Pennick. He would moan and complain—but if the goods were there, he'd deliver. Ten minutes—he was back on the line.

'Referedce Gederal Braddod,' he croaked. 'Iditial

applicatiod frob US Arby—dated February ted.'

'Ten?'

'Ted. Thad's whad I said.'

'Who signed it?'

A pause. 'W Cordhill, Major.'

'*Cornhill?*'

'*C-O-R-N-H-I-L-L . . . Cordhill.* Anythig else?'

I tried a long shot. 'How about something from the same source—later . . . April–May time?'

It paid off.

'*. . . I am instructed to inform you that a signal has been received here this morning indicating that the exhumation of General Brandon's body was satisfactorily completed yesterday and to thank you, Sir. . . .*'

The letter, addressed to the Right Honorable Chuter Ede—then Home Secretary—was sent from Camp Ajax, Pennsylvania on Wednesday April 16, 1947 and signed *W Cornhill, Major.*

I returned to the lounge. '*One checked out beautifully; then there were two.*'

Cornhill was on his feet. 'Doctor Meynell, I *insist* you tell me what you know. Fairfield's going to be hit by this affair—but at least give us a chance to co-operate. If we can stand up and say we helped bring this man to court, that will be some kind of answer to all those critics who want to label us a bunch of crooks.'

'How far is Hatchfield from Reverence?'

'*Huh?*'

I repeated the question. He clearly regarded it as irrelevant. 'It's just up the road,' he said. 'Eighteen

. . . twenty miles. What—?'

'Foster Durrell—d'you know how he spent the war?'

'No.' He spoke petulantly but immediately regained his composure. '*Yes*. He was at a training base in Florida. Army Air Force. Are you suggesting—?'

I looked into his troubled eyes. 'Bear with me, Mr Cornhill. I have a choice to make. If I get it wrong. . . .'

For two silent minutes I weighed what we knew. Then I decided. Walter Cornhill was watching me closely.

'When does Foster Durrell arrive?' I asked.

CHAPTER
FOURTEEN

When I was a child *Alice Through The Looking Glass* gave me nightmares. The Tenniell illustrations were grim enough but the thesis was grimmer. To be a pawn in a bizarre game of chess was a terrifying prospect. And now the nightmare was real—with one vital difference. Far from being a mere pawn in the game I was a threatened king. *Uneasy lies the head.* . . . Kendrick, Piper and Peters had all been powerful pieces—made strong by the knowledge they possessed. So they had been taken. Art Morino, a pawn unwittingly shielding my square in an evil moment, went the same way—lifted from the board and tossed aside.

Away in the Philippines that July day, chessmasters Karpov and Korchnoi were limbering up for a contest in which games would be won, lost and drawn. In *this* end game I faced a man who could not settle for stalemate. His every move had been aggressive, forcing me onto the defensive. But the night's events hinted lack of caution. Could we tempt him? I thought of Myra's father, crossing the wide Atlantic as a bishop moves diagonally over chequered squares. Another powerful piece. Set knight and king beside his episcopal lordship and. . . ? Meek and I set out for London Airport.

We went openly, lingering at the kerb for the benefit of watchful eyes. And we travelled in Meek's customized Mini-Cooper—a dazzling all-white package of power and gadgetry.

Five minutes on the motorway—crawling at thirty in the slow lane—and Meek gave a satisfied grunt. 'Company.'

A glance through the rear window showed me stream of traffic spaced out behind. 'Sure?'

'I know my job, squire. Grey Merk. Speed we're going, he should have passed us, way back. Give him a run if you like.'

He pulled into the fast lane and stayed there for a mile, then we were back cruising at forty. Behind us a grey Mercedes saloon slid out of sight beyond a Shell tanker.

'Doesn't *have* to be our man,' I said cautiously.

'The thought had occurred. Could be the Old Man's checking up on us. He has this thing about what he calls my *excesses*—and he did tell you to stay by a phone.'

I pointed to the smart green carphone clamped beneath his instrument panel. He grinned. 'That's unofficial. His Eminence doesn't know—*Hang about*!' His glance had flicked to the mirror again. 'Here comes trouble.'

I looked over my shoulder and saw the Mercedes moving up fast in the outside lane. 'He won't risk anything here.'

He prodded the release catch of my seatbelt. '*Get down!*'

I got—sliding forward . . . knees bent . . . back

arched . . . head pressed against the body-warm lambs-wool seat cover. A minute passed . . . very slowly.

'Clear,' said Meek, and I eased myself up.

'You saw him?'

'Bombing past at ninety? Oh sure, I saw a *lot*—like . . . he's white.' A hand reached for the carphone. 'Got his number, though.'

'If you're thinking of checking it with the Department—forget it.' I refastened my seatbelt. 'You said yourself it could be a Ministry car. We call in now . . . there'll be questions. Next thing—they're telling us to break off and get back home to mother. Let's wait—see if he turns up again.'

Meek's eyes narrowed. 'If he's a pro he'll know we've sussed him. *Might* just try the old dodge—pull off at an intersection and wait for us—but my guess is he knows where we're headed. If the Old Bill don't pull him in for speeding, he'll be at the airport. Y'know, squire—I don't think this trip is such a good idea.'

At Heathrow Central Area Durrell's flight arrival was being announced as we got out of the car. A uniformed airport constable bore down on us. 'Can't leave that there.' An imperious hand indicated the Mini. Meek stooped to breathe in his ear and show an ID wallet—a quick flash, surreptitious as a bribe. Then we were away through the glass doors.

'Get them to check the passenger list,' I said. 'Make certain he was on this flight.'

'But he's in the clear. Cornhill says he spent the war at a training base in Florida. And if he's on this flight—'

'Exactly. *If*. When he comes down those steps I

want to be sure he's travelled all the way from Reverence.'

He hesitated, his brown eyes troubled. 'Don't like leaving you alone.'

'We can't stand around holding hands. He'll be through any minute. I know what he looks like—you don't. Get your skates on.'

Naked to mine enemies—the way I felt after he had gone. Knotted stomach . . . tense shoulders—and an attack of the shakes which must have made me a blurred target. The concourse was an overturned anthill seething with bewildered humanity. Here solemn faces of parting friends; there an exuberant group caught up in the square-dance of reunion . . . and anywhere—anywhere at all—the questing eyes of a man who wanted me dead. I kept moving, using the crowd as cover yet never allowing myself to be trapped in its surging press. Memory recalled a man shot at close range during rush-hour on the Paris *Metro*, carried along for fifty yards—his dead body held erect by the insensitive log-jam of commuters. A cautionary sight.

Meek was on his way back, swimming chin-high through a sea of black homburgs as a crowd of earnest young orthodox Jews crossed his path.

'All serene,' he said briskly. 'He was on the flight. Ticket booked weeks ago.'

And there was Durrell—flightbag in one hand, briefcase in the other, a lightweight rainproof slung over his shoulder. We caught up with him by the entrance. As I touched his arm he spun round in alarm.

'*What*—? Why, it's Doctor Meynell!' He dropped the flightbag and reached out to grip my hand. 'What's this—a reception committee?' A nervous smile twitched his cheeks.

I nodded. 'By arrangement with Walter Cornhill.'

'No kidding! Well, I don't know what I've done to deserve this honour but I'm sure glad to see you. This place has changed since last time I was over!'

Meek stooped to pick up the flightbag. 'Let's not stand around,' he muttered, moving off towards the car.

'Meek's with me on the Kendrick case,' I explained.

Durrell stared. 'You're still working on it? But . . . after Myra spoke with you the other day I called Vincent in New York and he was dead against having you involved. Sore, I guess—the way you'd turned him down. And he reckoned Peters was out of line, approaching you after we'd taken him off the case.'

While Meek stowed his bag, Durrell walked slowly round the Mini as if viewing a rare exhibit—measuring it with his eye and shaking his head in amused disbelief. We burrowed awkwardly onto the rear seat and settled ourselves as Meek slid behind the wheel and switched on the stereo cassette player.

'How is Myra?' I asked, above the *Close Encounters* theme.

Durrell shook his head. 'She's a brave girl, Doctor. Too brave—know what I mean? So I'm old-fashioned, but I'd be easier in my mind if I saw a few tears. Doesn't do to hold things in the way she's doing.'

We moved off slowly, squeezing between a double row of taxis like a wary white mouse among hostile black cats. Durrell leaned back clutching his brief-case—a worried frown on his face. 'She's been hit hard,' he said. 'Okay, so you might not think so, the way she held up at the funeral—but don't let that fool you. And she's going to be hurt again. Hell—I wish I could have seen Vincent before this trip started. He'd know what to do. But—what am I saying? *You're* just the man! Here—what d'you make of this?'

He thrust a hand inside his jacket . . . paused—and suddenly a bewildered frown creased his forehead. 'My papers!' he gasped. 'They're gone! And my pass-port. I had them back there.' He grabbed Meek's shoulder. 'Hold it. I must have left them at the desk. Turn around.'

'No chance.' Meek shook off the clutching hand. 'We're on a one-way lane. I'll pull in; you nip back.' He stopped the car, scrambled out and tilted his seat forward. Clutching his briefcase, Durrell eased him-self through the door, took a couple of steps towards the terminal building—then stopped. I saw him open the case and peer inside. Then he turned, relief on his face. He spoke, but the words were lost in the roar of jets lifting a blue and white giant from the runway.

Back in the car he gave a short humourless laugh. 'Not like me to make that kind of mistake—but this damn business. . . .' He was jerked back as Meek let in the clutch and hurled the Mini forward in a racing start, screaming up through the gears at a rate of one every other second. Durrell glanced nervously out of the window. 'Say—do we have to go this fast?'

Meek was enjoying himself. 'Fast? Just an illusion,

man. Comes from being closer to the ground.'

I caught his eye in the mirror . . . frowned—and felt the speed drop. Fifty. Durrell relaxed. 'Sorry if I seem jittery, Doctor, but this business has been going round and round inside my head for days—and no-one to talk it over with. It's really getting to me.'

He fumbled with the flap of his old fashioned briefcase—veteran of many a boardroom campaign. Worn leather, faded gold initials, patched corners and cordbound handle implied wisdom and experience above and beyond the natty executive/overnight brigade. An essay in one-upmanship.

'Ah!' Groping fingers fastened on a sheet of paper. 'Here it is—the little timebomb I've uncovered. What d'you make of *that*?'

It was a handwritten list. As I frowned at the blurred words, Anne's voice sounded in my mind: 'Your *glasses*, David!' I found them.

1. Monet. Picasso.
2. Triton. Chalice.
3. Van Gogh. Vase.
4. Monstrance.
5. Miniatures. Jade.
6. Ikon!!

Timebomb? I looked questioningly at Durrell. 'A list of the stolen property?'

He pointed. 'See the way they're grouped?'

'That's significant?'

'To you—maybe not. Found this in Matt's desk when I was helping Myra sort his things. It's his writing. Knew it was trouble, soon as I saw it. Six groups—right? Forget the last one. That ikon was Matt's. So—five groups left. That tell you anything?'

'Five people?'

He nodded. 'That's the way I see it. And I guess I don't need to say *which* five. Now take group Two—*Triton . . . Chalice*. Mine. The only other group I'm sure about is *One*. Vincent. He owns that blue Picasso. Group Five *could* be Paul. Jade. He's into oriental stuff. But group *Four* is the one. There it is—the vase; the thing we all deny owning.'

I indicated the item beside it. 'Van Gogh. Who owns that?'

He spread his hands. 'Doctor—I'm no connoisseur. Once in a while I buy an antique because it's going to be worth a whole lot more when I sell. That blue Picasso thing I remember because I've seen it at Vincent's place and it stuck in my mind—but as for the rest. . . .'

'Surely you remember who claimed *what* when the stuff was recovered.'

'We didn't sit around comparing notes. The police had us in separately to identify our own property. That's why I wanted to check with Vincent before I came over here. *He'd* know. Matt used to say we were all—what's the word?—*Philistines*. Me?—sure, I don't mind admitting it. But not Vincent. That man has a real interest in art. If he's seen that Van Gogh hanging on a wall up on Olivet he'll remember *where*. But you see the position I'm in. I can show this list to you—but who else? Who can I trust? Say I show it to Walter here in London and it turns out *he's* the one. . . .'

'*We have company.*' Meek spoke calmly, his voice just audible above the taped music. 'Our friend's back. Keeping his distance three hundred yards behind. Lose him?'

'No—he's where we want him.' I pointed to the carphone. 'Call my wife. The number's—'

'I know the number, squire.' He had already pulled the green handset from its rest.

I faced Durrell. 'You don't have to worry about Walter Cornhill. He's not the man we're after. But I'll ask him about the Van Gogh. It'll confirm what I already know.'

He stared in amazement. 'You *know*? You know who killed Matt?'

It was a moment to savour. 'Matt . . . Ollie Piper in Reverence; Peters and a man called Morino, here in London. Yes—I know who he is, and *where* he is. He's back there, following us in a grey Mercedes.'

Durrell twisted round to stare through the rear window, then looked me straight in the eyes as the full import of my words registered. '*Peters?* You said *Peters* is dead? But—'

'*Your wife on the line.*' Meek handed me the phone, its coiled cable stretched taut across the front seat.

'Anne? We're on our way back.'

'So I gather.' Her voice was warm. 'Durrell checked out?'

'But of course. More important, you-know-who is on our tail—so we'll work things the way we planned.'

'Richmond Park? You *will* take care. Meek knows what to do?'

I chuckled. 'Meek always knows what to do. Put Cornhill on, will you?'

A moment later the lawyer was on the line. 'Everything okay, Doctor?'

'Looking good—but we're coming up to the dodgy bit. I'll feel better when that's over. A question: that Van Gogh—the one Matt lifted. Whose is it?'

His reply came without a moment's hesitation. 'It's mine.'

He was not supposed to say that.

Beside me, Durrell's agitated fingers drummed his briefcase. I stared—my mind racing. We had been so *wrong*. Blind . . . *deaf*. Deaf to what Dan Peters had told us in his last dying whisper. Walter Cornhill's voice broke in on my bewildered thoughts. 'Is it important?'

'Huh?'

'My Van Gogh—is it important?'

'I . . . I'm not sure. Ask me that in an hour's time. 'bye.'

I handed the phone to Meek—saw him replace it. 'Change of plan,' I said. 'Take us home.' Our eyes met in the mirror.

'Well?' Durrell seemed to sense my confusion. 'What did he say? Who owns the Van Gogh?'

I pulled off my glasses and looked at him helplessly. '*He* does.'

'My God!' His hands gripped the briefcase. 'Walter? But . . . I've known him thirty years. I . . . I just don't know what to say.'

That made two of us. I had been so confident—secure in the belief that I knew the identity of the killer; priding myself on our plan to lead him to Richmond Park—hunter's terrain where Meek's telescopic rifle would outmatch a 38 and bring Effendi to heel. Now that confidence was shattered. I turned to Durrell. 'We're going to my apartment. Cornhill's there. He won't expect us so soon—but just remember my wife is with him. He only has to threaten her and our advantage is gone. So we play it cool.'

He nodded but his face had hardened. 'Thirty years,' he muttered. 'I respected him . . . *trusted* him. What kind of man *is* he? At the funeral . . . all that sympathy for Myra—and he's the one who made a widow of her.'

Meek said, 'If Cornhill's our man—who's that on our tail?'

I glanced back at the grey Mercedes, still pacing us three hundred yards behind. 'Ministry watchdog. Has to be.'

I caught his reflected frown. 'If you say so, squire. Ask me, you're making too much of that scrap of paper. Could be a plant.'

'Think I haven't considered that?' Durrell demanded wretchedly. 'I've tried convincing myself it's a forgery but that just doesn't add up. I only found it by chance in Matt's desk diary. Could have stayed hidden for months . . . years. Where's the sense in planting something that might never be found? And it's Matt's writing—that's for sure.'

'Who told us Cornhill was clear?' asked Meek pointedly. 'Who said—?'

'Just shut up will you?' I was trying to think and time was running out.

We came off the motorway heading east along Chiswick High Road, down King Street and into a long tailback of traffic crawling past a minor shunt on Hammersmith Broadway—a lorry, a taxi and a blue Capri. Glass everywhere . . . one man sitting dazed on the kerb—but nobody seriously hurt. As we crept past I looked back. Close behind, a heavy lorry blocked the view, airbrakes hissing impatiently; but I glimpsed the Mercedes reflected in a showroom window across the street. Then the police were waving us on and we were away down Hammersmith Road with the vast bulk of Olympia coming up on our left. Nearly home.

'Back door?' asked Meek as we passed the end of Phillimore Gardens.

For a moment I hesitated. 'Front.'

So we came home. Scrambling from the car I spotted that other grey saloon pulling in to the kerb a hundred yards down the road.

Curtain up on the final act.

CHAPTER
FIFTEEN

We took the stairs—Meek first, Durrell at his heels. As we padded along the first landing I saw the gun in Meek's hand.

'Put that thing away,' I hissed but as I followed them up the next flight I felt for the Beretta at my waist—safetycatch forward, thumb on the rough serrated cocking-lever, pulling it back. My jacket muffled that reassuring double click. By the apartment door I caught Durrell's arm and spoke in an urgent whisper. 'Remember—we suspect *nothing*. One word out of place could blow the whole thing.'

He was hugging his briefcase as if it offered security in a world gone mad. 'I don't think I can.' His voice was choked, his head shaking from side to side. He swallowed noisily. 'Leave me out of this. I'll wait here until—'

'Don't be a fool,' snapped Meek. 'He knows you're with us. Probably saw us all get out of the car. You stay out here and he'll guess something's wrong.'

'We're wasting time,' I said—and pushed my key in the door.

As we walked into the lounge Anne sprang up from the Chesterfield and ran towards me. 'It's over—already?'

'It hasn't started yet. Where's Cornhill?'

I saw the skin tighten at her temples as she caught the urgency in my voice. 'He's . . . he's in the bathroom. David—what's happened?'

'Get over there—the chair by the window.'

No more questions. She moved swiftly across the room and sat by the phone table. I looked at Durrell and pointed to one of the armchairs. He stumbled forward like a man in a daze and sank into the chair facing the window—his back to the door through which Cornhill must enter. Meek and I stood in the middle of the room . . . waiting.

Our clock chimed two quarters. Four-thirty. I had lost all sense of time.

Waiting. . .

In the stillness I caught distant rumbles of a cistern emptying and the hiss of water in the pipes—then the sound of Cornhill humming tunelessly as he came towards us along that short passage.

The door opened and he was in the room. His eyebrows lifted as he saw us. '*That* was quick. We hadn't expected—' He stopped, the smile fading. 'Trouble?'

I folded my arms, right hand groping for the Beretta. '*Trouble*. We picked up Mr Durrell as planned—'

He noticed the other man in the armchair. 'Why hello there, Foster. Have a good trip?'

Durrell's attempt at a smile resulted in a sickly leer. Cornhill stared. 'You all right, Foster?'

I looked at Durrell's twitching face and knew we could play this game no longer. 'About your Van

Gogh,' I said. 'You asked if it was important. Show him the list, Mr Durrell.'

The man in the chair seemed prey to conflicting emotions. His breathing was rapid, his face pale and anguished. He stared up at Cornhill with wild eyes. 'Yes,' he gasped. 'I'll show him.'

As he flipped open his briefcase and thrust his right hand deep among its contents I slid the Beretta from its holster. He stood up, still fumbling in the case. I caught his agitated muttering: *'Thirty years. Filthy murdering devil . . .'*

Cornhill tensed and in that instant his right hand flew to the pocket of his jacket. Time had run out. I fired.

Snap shooting—but at that range who could miss? The bullet drilled through that shabby briefcase as Durrell was lifting it higher. Time froze . . . then the case was falling. . . . As it hit the carpet a revolver shot out and clattered onto the marble hearth while Durrell clutched his shattered wrist and made inhuman mewing noises. I felt like a gambler who has staked everything—and just seen his number come up on the wheel. Cornhill was standing open-mouthed, freeze-framed in the act of pulling a glasses-case from his pocket. I dashed for the door, cannoning into the astonished Meek.

'Watch him!' I gasped.

He grabbed my arm. 'Where. . . ?'

I shook him off. 'The car! The car!' Then I was out on the landing, through the back entrance and taking those stone steps three at a time.

Courtyard . . . garage . . . corner . . . a short street

. . . another corner—and there was the Mercedes, fifteen yards ahead and facing away from me, its right side against the kerb.

Gasping for breath I prayed the driver would not look in the mirror. Ten yards. Five. I was level with the rear seat. The engine was purring softly but the driver had not moved.

'End of the line, Myra,' I said and put my gun to her head.

She turned and looked up at me, her eyes lost behind oversize sunglasses. 'You won't use that,' she said—and let in the clutch. As the car shot forward I grabbed for the door and felt the Beretta slip from my hand—then I was being dragged along, clinging to that door-frame as the Mercedes gained speed. Suddenly the door was thrust violently open. I lost my grip and fell heavily, rolling over and over towards the gutter. I heard the shriek of tyres and looked up to see the Mercedes slewed broadside across the road. Myra was out of the car and walking towards me. She seemed in no hurry—and there was something in her hand.

Struggling to my knees I tried to crawl for cover behind a parked van but it was like moving in a dream—my limbs molten lead. I heard her voice, clear . . . mocking—making play of my own words.

'End of the line—*Professor!*'

As I stared helplessly she raised the gun in her right hand. . . .

Then she shuddered, her head jerked sideways—and half her face just *fell off* in a crimson cascade.

She went down in an ungainly heap like a humanely

slaughtered beast in an *abattoir*. As the sound of a shot crackled down the street. . . .

'What a waste,' said Meek.

Late sunlight glinted gold on the western mosaics of the Albert Memorial. Across in the concert hall the LSO was tuning up while a few disconsolate would-be promenaders lingered beneath the arched portico— foolish virgins too late for the nuptials. Around us in Kensington Gardens youth sprawled on the grass while age walked slowly by—remembering. We sat on the warm lower steps of the Memorial—Anne, Meek and I—released at last from hours of interrogation in which police, MOD and some suave young men from the American Embassy had taken turn and turn about. We had been questioned separately in claustrophobic interview-rooms. Now under a blue sky flecked with pink-tinged clouds and vapour-trails there were still questions and—from Meek—recriminations.

'You could have told me. You pulled that gun on Durrell—I thought you'd flipped. Then you leave me standing there like a right charlie. *The car! The car!* What the hell was that supposed to mean? Lucky for you I came down. *Next* time—'

'There isn't going to be a next time. You saved my life. I'm grateful—but did you have to kill Myra Kendrick?'

'I had a choice? She was fifty feet away—pointing her little shooter at your nut.' He shook his head morosely. 'She had to go, squire. She *had* to go. If you'd told me what was happening, earlier. . . .'

'How? I guessed the truth when I was on the phone in your car but that wasn't the time or place to blurt it out. I had to find a way to make Durrell commit himself. He was obviously trying to throw suspicion on Walter Cornhill. I needed to know how far he was prepared to go.'

'And now you know. *All the way*. Another second and poor old Cornhill would have been a goner. You cut it fine.'

'I'd been so sure Grant Aitken was Effendi. Everything pointed to him—specially after Cornhill told us Durrell spent the war in Florida. That was Durrell's story to cover the fact that he was court-martialled after the crash in which General Brandon was killed. Guilty of negligence, shipped back to the States, ended up behind a desk at an Air Force training base.'

Anne leaned back against the step. 'I'm still in the dark. You tell me Durrell's made a statement and everything's sewn up—right?'

Meek was picking the blister on his palm. 'He's been singing like a canary. I thought it might help things along if he had a good look at his daughter before they scraped her off the street and cleaned up the mess. That's why I dragged him down straight away. I was right. Loosened his tongue a treat.'

Anne shivered and felt for my hand. 'Suppose we begin at the beginning. . . .'

It began with a young pilot scrambling from the wreckage of his Piper Cub to face an elderly Englishman in Norfolk tweeds. For two days Durrell stayed at Danton Court under the care of a local doctor—his delirious mutterings giving Annandale the story behind the crash. Removed to a military hospital he returned, hobbling on crutches, to express gratitude. It was the day of Italy's surrender. Annandale warmed to the young flier. That nickname—*Effendi*—was an accolade from a man who shrank from displays of friendship. Recalling his own youth he showed Durrell his old scarlet uniform. Then—in an ill-omened moment—he lifted the lid of a shabby trunk . . . and there was the Pompadour Vase.

The court-martial and its aftermath left indelible marks on Durrell. Iron entered his soul. A civilian again, he brought to Fairfield a ruthlessness which carried him to executive level. His carefully edited *curriculum vitae* had been purged of all reference to military service in Britain. Hatchfield—General Brandon's home—was just up the road, too close for a man held responsible for the general's death.

Married now, he began collecting antiques—buying and selling without regard for intrinsic value—profit his sole motive. Dealings became increasingly furtive as he was drawn into the twilight world of illegal art-trading.

Then, early in 1947, the Pompadour Vase came into his life again. In January the New York Times reported a record saleroom price paid by Oberon Spreight. Durrell cut the report from the paper and clipped it to Hugh Annandale's letter, still among souvenirs of a service career he dared not acknow-ledge. He began to dream of that vase as a stock-market gambler dreams of a quick killing.

From Walter Cornhill he learned of plans to exhume General Brandon's body for reburial in Hatchfield. Here was irony—a chance to benefit at the posthumous expense of a man whose impatient folly had blighted Durrell's flying career.

He travelled to England with only a loosely-formulated plan, ready to seize opportunity when it presented—the whole venture a gamble. Brandon's body, disinterred at dusk, would rest overnight in the parish church before being driven to Southampton for shipment aboard a transatlantic liner. Travelling by air Durrell could be back in Reverence while that ship was still on the high seas.

He anticipated no difficulty in forging an entrance to Danton Court and securing the vase. His only problem was its removal to the church, three-quarters of a mile distant. With petrol rationed he had been unable to rent a car. His only transport was a sit-up-and-beg cycle bought second-hand in Rugby. But fortune smiled—he met Paddy Power.

To the Irishman that American accent talked money. He offered the stranger what he claimed was a genuine Roman antiquity. Undeceived, Durrell paid the fifty pounds demanded, seeing it as an investment. Accepting, Power played into his hands. At a meeting next day—arranged to discuss possible future business—Durrell accused the airman of selling a worthless forgery and threatened to report him to the police. To avoid that, Power found himself agreeing to help with the operation planned for that night. He shrank from returning to Danton Court so soon after his encounter with Annandale's angry dog, but protest was useless.

In his statement made under interrogation Durrell stressed two points: the robbery was conceived on a purely *ad hoc* basis—leaving him free to abort the operation at any stage—and never at any time did he contemplate violence. Hindsight makes the true situation tragically clear. Recruiting that unwilling ally brought Durrell to the point of no return—and the moment Power learned of that operation, he became expendable.

The front door of Danton Court was unlocked; the house in darkness. Power's repeated warning of the owner's nocturnal vigilance left Durrell undeterred. Within minutes they were outside again, carrying the small trunk in which lay the Pompadour Vase. And there—as they crossed the gravel drive—they encountered Annandale with his elderly Alsatian on its leash.

Who struck the fatal blows? We have only Durrell's account and he swore that Power killed both man and dog. But where in the darkness would Power have found a weapon? *Durrell* came prepared for a break-in. His implements would be to hand. The jury may draw its own conclusions.

They left Annandale dead or dying and hurried to the church. Again, an unlocked door—no unusual thing in those days before vandalism became a cult. The place was deserted. Resting on two coffin-stools lay the large casket made by Hatchfield's leading undertaker at public expense. So generous were its proportions that the trunk could be fitted inside.

Once the coffin lid was refastened the only immediate problem was disposal of the bag containing
General Brandon's mortal residue. Again Durrell's
investment paid a dividend. Power remembered the
waterlogged pit he had helped to dig only a few days
previously. Retracing their steps over the bridge they
crept along the river bank keeping as far as possible
from Danton Court.

Maybe there—stumbling along in the darkness—
Durrell realised how vulnerable he would be if the
Irishman lived to see another dawn. In his statement
he speaks of an argument . . . of Power's threat of
blackmail . . . of a struggle on the edge of that dark
pit. Whatever the attendant circumstances, Power's
body entered the water in company with Brandon's
bones—weighted by the paving-stone which Durrell
fetched from where it lay hidden beside his cycle down
the lane.

The theft of the Pompadour Vase went unnoticed.
There were no signs of forcible entry—and no-one
knew what remained of Danton's treasures after the
years of the locust. Mrs Drumsell, in a state of shock,
was in no condition to assist the police with their
enquiries and by the time she was discharged from
hospital Annandale's furniture and effects had been
sold by order of his executors.

So came the second Pompadour Vase to America.
For five years it lay in the Brandon family vault.
Before Durrell could recover it, tragedy struck. His
wife died giving birth to their only child—Myra. To

the bereaved man it seemed vengeful fate had de-livered its riposte, thrusting at his heart.

But—inexorably—greed triumphed over grief. His thoughts turned again to that vault in Hatchfield.

The Brandon mausoleum was not built with an eye to security. It stood in a secluded corner of the cemetery, screened by trees— a replica in miniature of a Greek temple. Only a hinged wrought-iron grille stood between Durrell and his prize. A simple lock, easy to open; easy to secure again—the whole opera-tion completed within thirty minutes.

He brought the vase home, locked it in its strong-room—and deliberately put it from his mind. Linked with a double killing in England it was a very hot property needing time to cool. More—those years of inactivity had seen his closest contacts in the art world arrested and imprisoned. No longer in a seller's market he turned his thoughts to legitimate business and the upbringing of his daughter.

Myra—how did she come to feature in events which would bring her to untimely death in a Kensington street? For her, Durrell could do no wrong. Say she worshipped the man and you speak no more than truth. His strength of purpose . . . business acumen . . . ruthlessness—these for her were marks of divi-nity.

She thought to find such attributes in Matthew Kendrick. After their marriage, knowing herself mistaken, she despised him and turned once more to her childhood idol.

So to Matt's futile protest in the cause of Art for All. The Pompadour Vase was an unexpected bonus lifted by Ollie Piper in excess of zeal. But when he staggered from Durrell's home clutching it to his bosom, Myra Kendrick already knew of its existence. A lonely child, she had once crept unnoticed into her father's strongroom and there seen that elegant piece of porcelain.

With Vincent Goring determined to bring Matt to court, Durrell feared the consequences. The trial would be reported. A picture of that vase in the press or on television could prove disastrous. Entering Matt's hotel by the fire escape Durrell listened at the door of 310 . . . heard voices . . . waited . . . saw me leave. While I was in the elevator—up on the fourth floor—and Miss Wandowska was climbing the stairs he walked into 310, shot Matt with his silenced revolver, and left as he had come, by the fire escape.

Oberon Spreight's theory—that Kendrick was killed because of the vase—alerted Myra to the truth. She confronted her father and offered to help him. When Vincent Goring suggested I be called in to assist with the investigation, she voiced support for the idea. Why not? I would almost certainly refuse—and even were I to accept, David Meynell—professor of archaeology—would be no match for Foster Durrell and his daughter.

It was Myra in that dark green Cadillac. Hurriedly briefed by her father she excused herself from her guests, drove to the address Peters had given, and used Foster Durrell's silenced gun on Ollie Piper. Only when she called me did she learn that Peters had damaging new evidence. She hung up and hurried to her father. New evidence pointing to Danton Court?

What had Peters found? Durrell recalled that letter—kept to establish the Pompadour Vase's *provenance* in the event of an illicit deal. Whatever Annandale had written—after so long Durrell could not remember details—one thing was certain: that letter must be destroyed together with anyone who had learned its secret. Myra would concentrate on Peters; I was to be Durrell's quarry. A quick dash to Hampton University was too dangerous. He might be recognised, his car registration recorded by a scrupulous police officer. In London he would be anonymous. He packed his flightbag.

Next day he was aboard a DC10 bound for England—only hours behind Anne and me. From London he called Myra and learned when Peters would arrive on Saturday—information supplied by Peters' unsuspecting secretary.

At London Airport he watched the investigator board an airline bus for the West London Terminal. Durrell had done his homework. His rented Mercedes raced the bus to its set-down point in Cromwell Road where Peters consulted a street guide and then walked the two blocks to Burgoyne Towers Hotel. There—in the room reserved by Oberon Spreight—Durrell shot him and retrieved Annandale's letter together with the clip from the New York Times.

Now he faced a problem—the conference with ICI scheduled for Tuesday there in London. In his haste he had forgotten vital documents. His ticket for the Monday flight from New York—booked weeks ahead—was at home in Reverence. He called Myra . . . told her to collect the documents and use his ticket to bring them to England. The future seemed secure.

Then he remembered—I must have seen Annandale's letter. Once more that ruthless streak asserted itself and in the early hours of Monday morning he came a-visiting—only to squander the life of Art Morino. Back at his hotel—a *very* discreet establishment where few questions were asked and fewer answered—he heard from a very worried Myra. She was calling from New York airport where her London flight was due—and she had disturbing news. Vincent Goring was claiming that Peters lived long enough to give me a vital lead on the man who shot him. But all was not lost. She would be bringing a desperately-devised plan which, if they kept their nerve, could turn seeming defeat into victory. No time for details. Meet her at London Airport.

One question tormented Durrell—*How much did I know?* With time to kill before Myra's arrival he drove the Mercedes to Kensington and parked in Tichborne Terrace where he could watch our apartment. Like the chess-player I pictured him to be, he was striving to anticipate my next move.

Walter Cornhill's arrival worried him. What were we discussing? Was the lawyer unwittingly tightening the net round Durrell and his daughter?

As he sat sweltering in that grey car the strain of recent events took full toll. Constant tension . . . little sleep—and now, gnawing uncertainty. The futility of it all! Matt Kendrick . . . Ollie Piper . . . Peters—their deaths had only postponed the day of reckoning. Myra had spoken of a scheme—but what could possibly redeem the situation now? His flightbag, ready packed, lay on the back seat. He could drive to the airport, meet her—and get out while there was time.

And at that moment of indecision Meek and I emerged from the apartment block and drove away. Where? Durrell *had* to know. As we hit the M4 he guessed. Heathrow. Cornhill must have told us the time his flight was due in.

Immediately hope rekindled. *If we believed he was flying in from New York, we could not suspect he had been in London for the past sixty hours.* Jacket collar up, hat low over his eyes, he pulled into the fast lane and went past us like the wind.

As Myra came through immigration he dragged her out of sight and in five fateful minutes they laid their plans. Her scheme had the simplicity of desperation. *Give me the daggers.* If suspicion could not be allayed it might yet be diverted. She had prepared a list of the stolen property in Matt's handwriting, designed to persuade us that Walter Cornhill was the man we sought. But Cornhill must not live to prove his innocence.

Durrell protested. To kill Cornhill in cold blood would mean years in a British prison. With inherited ruthlessness Myra urged him to face facts. Given extenuating circumstances—and Durrell must provide those by appearing overwrought . . . shattered by Cornhill's guilt—the charge could be manslaughter. Better that than life as fugitives or a charge of multiple murder involving father and daughter. He recognised the logic and braced himself as she handed him the briefcase containing his conference documents.

Hastily he slipped his gun into the case. Myra had brought her own automatic. He approved the scheme but as a final precaution insisted she be at hand with the Mercedes. If things went wrong, flight would be their only option. Quickly he described Meek's car, promising to delay us long enough for her to get on its tail—the pretence of lost papers and passport; the querulous plea for reduced speed. Then he passed her the keys of the Mercedes, told her where it was parked and left, to mingle with the last of the passengers from the flight on which he was supposed to have arrived.

So he came hurrying across the concourse—an innocent man in our eyes. We had the airline's assurance that he had travelled on that aircraft but the busy clerk had checked reservation dockets not faces. We were blind to the possibility that Myra had substituted for Durrell.

The story—thirty-five years in the writing—moved to its climax.

I slid an arm round Anne's waist. 'And that's it. You know the rest.'

'Don't you play games with me, David Meynell.' Her hand gripped my chin, forcing my head round. 'Look at me when I'm talking to you. You know perfectly well you've missed out the important bit.'

'I *have*?'

'You didn't know any of this when you pulled out your gun in the apartment this afternoon. You took a terrible risk. What made you suspect Durrell?'

'Oh *that*.' I leaned back on the steps, pulling her down beside me. 'He told me.'

'Stop teasing!'

'He *did*. He spelled it out for me—easy as *A-B-C*. It was in the car. I'd just asked Cornhill who owned that Van Gogh—thinking he'd say Grant Aitken, the man who was over here with the Eighth Air Force during the war. When he said it was *his* . . . well—I just sat there trying to sort out what that meant. Durrell was fiddling with his briefcase—tapping his fingers on it. I had my glasses on by then so I could see what I hadn't noticed before.' I stopped—picturing the scene and marvelling that Durrell should have been betrayed by his own hand.

'Go on,' urged Anne.

'Remember what Peters said when he was dying? He said *Effendi*. He said it very slowly, as if he was afraid I wouldn't understand. I said Yes, it was the name we'd seen in that letter. Remember what he said then? *'No. You don't see. Here.'* It cost him a tremendous effort to get those words out. What d'you suppose he meant?'

She sat up, frowning. 'He was telling you that Effendi wasn't just a name in a letter—that he was here in London.'

'Exactly what I thought—but I was wrong. He wasn't saying *here H-E-R-E* . . . he was saying *hear H-E-A-R*. Get it? *Effendi*—you don't *see* it, you *hear* it. That was our trouble. We'd seen it written down and that put us on the wrong track. And *that's* what I saw on Durrell's briefcase. His initials. Foster Norman Durrell—*F.N.D.*'

* * *

After the interrogations—the horse-trading. Durrell was extradited for trial in Reverence on the charge of murdering Matthew Kendrick. A weak case—as District Attorney Cook acknowledged privately. On a Not Guilty plea he might have been acquitted. When the hearing came up, two British police officers were in court and further extradition papers had already been prepared.

He pleaded Guilty.

No mention was made of General Brandon at the trial. His remains were secretly reburied in Hatchfield. Maybe silence was part of the deal—I don't know. What I *do* know is, if Durrell lives to complete his sentence, two discreet Englishmen will again be waiting as he steps from the state penitentiary. The flight to London should be quicker by then. And I'm sure we'll be hearing of General Brandon at the Old Bailey.

We stood in the deserted apartment, stripped now of all its furnishing. Anne gazed round at the unfamiliar emptiness. 'The next people here,' she whispered, '—they'll never know how it was for us.'

'Best that way.' My voice sounded hollow . . . sepulchral. 'If they've any sense they'll leave the past alone.'

We closed the door softly and hurried down to where the removers were stacking our future in their van.

OUR RECORD
OF PREVIOUS CRIMES

Some of the exciting tales of murder, mystery, danger, detection and suspense already published in Keyhole Crime.

Look out for them wherever you normally buy paperbacks

 Keyhole Crime

NOW READ ON WITH KEYHOLE CRIME
Other titles available in the shops now

LETTER OF INTENT
Ursula Curtiss

When Celia Brett plans to marry and complete her ruthless climb to the top of New England society she receives a letter that threatens to blow her carefully constructed world to pieces.

RANSOM TOWN
Peter Alding

Detective Inspector Fusil fights against time to track down the Organisation for Social Equality who is demanding payment to halt its relentless campaign of arson.

THE BURGLAR IN THE CLOSET
Lawrence Block

In the course of thieving the New York apartment of beautiful Crystal Sheldrake, Bernie Rhodenbarr, professional burglar, not only loses his swag but becomes implicated in murder.

 Keyhole Crime

A FEW CLUES ABOUT MORE GREAT TITLES YOU'LL SOON BE SEEING IN KEYHOLE CRIME

WYCLIFFE AND THE PEAGREEN BOAT
W. J. Burley

The Cornish village had been celebrating Coronation Carnival week when Alice Weekes was found raped and strangled on a cliff top shortly after she had been seen with Morley Tremain.

Twenty-one years later Chief Superintendent Wycliffe is investigating the cruel murder of Morley's uncle in the same village. The old man's son is charged, but Wycliffe finds that there is a vital link between the two cases.

CATCH-AS-CATCH-CAN
Charlotte Armstrong

Laila's father whisks her off from a small Pacific island to the hills of California. She had never been to school, can hardly write her name and is left totally naive and defenceless when her father dies.

One summer's day she eats some poisoned beans and, ignorant of the fatal implications, she runs away and has to be found *before midnight* or death will take her hand.

 Keyhole Crime

DOWN AMONG THE DEAD MEN
Evelyn Harris

When six-year-old Dixon Taggard went missing,
Stephen Brand had no inclination to go scouring the
countryside for him. But when he did begin looking
he discovered all kinds of worrying details about a
briefcase Dixon had found and some strange men
seen loitering around the village in a watchful,
menacing way.
Then the little boy was found dead — and his death
was not the last . . .

THE DEAD SIDE OF THE MIKE
Simon Brett

The death of Studio Manager Andrea Gower looked
like suicide, but curiously enough she was sitting very
recently in a BBC bar with actor Charles Paris and
chatting about her career and hopes for the future —
quite obviously in high spirits.
Charles is determined to prove a case of murder and
following a series of clues that nearly leads to his own
death, uncovers a complicated fraud inside the
hallowed portals of Broadcasting House.